THE SIEGE OF BLACKBRAE

The Gateway series:

and other titles

The Siege of Blackbrae

by
CHRIS SAVERY

LUTTERWORTH PRESS
Guildford Surrey England

First published 1971
Reprinted 1981

Copyright © 1971 Lutterworth Press
All Rights Reserved

ISBN 0 7188 1879 2

PRINTED IN GREAT BRITAIN
BY MACKAYS OF CHATHAM LTD

Contents

Chapter 1

THE PATAGONIAN AFFAIR

MOST people, it is said, have a skeleton in a cupboard. Robin Chesney and Howard Hunt shared one, not a grinning skull and bare bones, but an unpleasant memory which they tried hard to keep locked up and out of sight. Their skeleton in the cupboard was the Patagonian Affair.

It had all happened three years ago, a kids' adventure which they had undertaken together and which did not turn out according to plan. Nobody likes to be reminded of the most foolish escapades of one's early days. It is downright unfair to unearth boobs made by boys not yet in their teens, though the misdoings of teenagers are fair game.

Their parents blamed the B.B.C. of course. Television is a convenient whipping-boy for youthful misdemeanours. An exciting T.V. series about travel in South America certainly did set the two boys dreaming of that amazing continent, though they would never have thought of visiting it if Tom Hopkins had not come along with his treasure map.

Tom Hopkins was to blame. Tom Hopkins put the idea into the heads of Robin Chesney and Howard Hunt. Tom Hopkins had quick wits and clever fingers and his bad spelling made the map look as if it was the real thing.

Robin's father was out of work at the time, having lost his job when the factory was ruined after a prolonged strike. Nobody need starve in a Welfare State, and the Chesney family were not exactly on the rocks, yet there was a feeling at home that a bit more cash in the kitty would not come amiss. Old Grandma Chesney, who liked her comforts, did a good deal of grumbling about Uncle Joseph, a man who was rich and could afford many things the Chesneys had to do without. Grandma's complaints might have been ignored, had it not been for the reading at school of *Treasure Island*, which is an inspiration for any adventurous boy to go treasure-seeking.

Howard Hunt read *Treasure Island* too. His people had no need of money. His mother and father both held good teaching posts. But Howard was a latch-key boy. He always arrived home after school before his parents, and he spent many lonely hours watching television by an electric fire or reading all by himself. He had to get his own tea and he often wished for a crowd of brothers and sisters. The wild loneliness of Patagonia and the turbulent seas dashing round Cape Horn did not impress him at all and he would not have dreamed of going to such a weird part of the world alone. But with his friend Robin Chesney he would have circumnavigated the globe, and he very nearly did.

Because along came Tom Hopkins with his treasure map.

The map was drawn in faded ink on aged parchment. Young Hopkins declared it to be the chart of a Portuguese explorer who had buried in Patagonia the loot he had pirated from a Spanish treasure ship, gold and jewels which, said Hopkins, the dagos had in their turn stolen from the royal family of the Incas. Attacked by a third pirate (the world was full of pirates in those days), the Portuguese explorer had surrendered his map in exchange for his life, to an Englishman named Anthony Hopkins, living on his ill-gotten gains during the reign of Elizabeth I, at about the time when Drake was sailing round the world. This Hopkins, ancestor of our Thomas at the West Tooting Comprehensive School, had been lost at sea but had left his map in an old sea-chest at home which Tom had discovered when turning out the family junk-room during spring cleaning. Rats had eaten the ship's log-book and damp had mouldered the diaries, but the map Tom passed with pride to Robin and Howard.

"If you could believe a tale like that, you could believe anything," said Tom when later accused of leading his friends astray. "It was only a joke. I drew the map myself on a bit of parchment from an old lampshade which my mum was going to throw away. If Chesney and Hunt had had one grain of sense between them, they would have checked up Patagonia on a school atlas before sailing off to Russia like two mad goons."

Of course they had not meant to go to Russia, they knew perfectly well that Patagonia was west and Russia east; but they happened to stow away on the wrong ship, having made inquiries from a sailor who was not to be trusted. They were both extremely sea-sick and had to give themselves up in the end, which was a terrifying experience, since none of the crew spoke English and the Russian language is apt to sound like a severe reprimand to those who cannot understand it.

When the sight of the Hammer and Sickle convinced them at last of their mistake in navigation, Robin and Howard were cast into utter despair. The ship had gone too far to turn back, and they proceeded on their way. The Russians, Howard whispered to Robin, have the reputation of grabbing any stray aliens and of keeping a firm hold on them, in order to turn them into Communists. Robin was more practical than Howard, but he had not read so widely, and he swallowed Howard's lurid descriptions of life in the U.S.S.R., becoming more and more alarmed as they tossed through northern waters towards the shadowy horror of the Iron Curtain.

They would be deported as spies to Siberia, Howard said, and his view of Siberia was that of a vast country with nothing in it but wolf packs (ravening wolves!), internment camps for all who rebel or try to escape, top-secret space travel installations, and here and there a gigantic crater caused by wandering meteorites.

In fact the Russians were not at all grasping. They were only too anxious to get rid of a couple of naughty boys who were a nuisance to all concerned. When they were landed, the Russians fed their stowaways with tea and bread and butter and put them into the next aeroplane going to Britain. They saw nothing of the country, which was wrapped in snow, the grub was nothing to boast about even in the air, and they felt too sick and miserable to enjoy the flight home.

Their arrival at Heathrow was ignominious. News was scarce at that time and bored reporters waiting for something to fill the T.V. screens and the newspapers got hold of the deportation of two schoolboys from Russia and they made the most of it. Like two lost dogs Howard and Robin shuffled down the gangway to meet their distracted parents. Lost dogs would have been much more fortunate, for they would have been popped immediately into quarantine kennels and forgotten about until all was forgiven and forgotten, but Robin and Howard had to endure a welcome heralded by flashing photographs and futile questions. And that evening all their acquaintances gawping at the television saw Robin being kissed by his weeping mother and Howard receiving a stern admonition from his schoolmaster father. Robin's dad gave him a hiding when he reached home, but afterwards never referred again to the incident. Howard's parents did not apply corporal punishment but they were not so good at forgetting as the Chesneys (not counting Grandma Chesney who had a sharp tongue and a long memory).

Stowing away on a ship is theft, stealing a passage. The returning of stowaways requires payment, and air fares are expensive. In consideration of youthful high spirits and its being a first offence, the Juvenile Court let them off lightly, but not so the West Tooting Comprehensive School!

The Headmaster gave them a talking-to and the rest of the staff was fairly decent on the whole, apart from a few sarcasms. But the boys and girls of the West Tooting Comprehensive were by no means so amiable. Sob-stuff and pathetic promises of "I'll never do it again" may take in a head-master, but not one's classmates.

Howard Hunt and Robin Chesney were fair game for ridicule and they got it. They were teased by their friends, tormented by their foes, ragged by parties completely unknown, for the school held over two thousand pupils.

"Red Robin and Comrade How" they were nicknamed.

"How do you hunt for treasure in Patagonia?" asked a passing senior.

"Pass me the caviare and the vodka, comrade," some ass would say at school dinner.

"Yo ho ho and a bottle of rum!" they quoted.

"Up the Jolly Roger, pirates all!" giggled the girls.

"Did you call at the Kremlin? Did you sail round Cape Horn?" someone would inquire.

Stupidest of all and the most irritating were the kids from the Primary School who got the story all wrong and joined in the joke by continually shouting after the returned adventurers:

"Two toads totally tired tried to trot to Turkey!" or even worse:

> "From Tooting they travelled to Spain,
>   They were dreadfully sick in the train,
>   Not once and again
>   But again and again
>   And again and again and again."

Robin and Howard never went near Turkey or Spain. They were sea-sick, not train-sick, and the insults were quoted wrongly too, but tormenters rarely worry about facts. The streets near the schools of Tooting echoed with jeers.

For a while only. Jokes become boring after a while and by the end of the long holidays most of their schoolfellows had forgotten the Patagonian affair. An occasional bit of leg-pulling, that was all. Robin Chesney and Howard Hunt did not forget, though. They were acutely conscious that they had boobed, and they dragged on a miserable existence for months under the mistaken impression that everyone despised them. Nobody despised them at all in fact but all the world loves a joke, though it takes a wise man to know when a joke ceases to be funny.

The Hopkins family moved to Carlisle at the beginning of the summer holidays and as far as his former friends knew, Tom was quit of the whole business. He had played a practical joke and taken the mickey out of his pals.

Robin and Howard drifted apart. They felt less conspicuous each on his own. Tom Hopkins, their tormenter-in-chief had gone but other wags remained. Robin threw himself with fervour into the sports side of school life and Howard pursued a lonely course, spending his free time in the library. He did not mind losing the treasure of the Incas, but he hated losing his two friends.

Eventually the Chesney family with Grandma moved to Norwich. Soon afterwards Howard's parents took excellent teaching posts in Bristol. The West Tooting Comprehensive School saw the three adventurers no more.

Carlisle in the North, Bristol in the South-West and East Anglia for Norwich. Three cities nicely separated far apart. The boys seemed well cut off from everything connected with that foolish escapade. For nobody remembers for long the odd incidents of news and the odder faces of the persons who appear on the television screen. Nobody hoards the indistinct pictures from old newspapers. That youthful mischief was dead and buried, never to be exhumed.

Or was it?

"When shall we three meet again?" asked the witches in *Macbeth*.

"In thunder, lightning or in rain?"

The Patagonian affair was not forgotten. Three years later the whirligig of time brought the three boys together once more.

Chapter 2

KEEP IT UNDER YOUR HAT

"ROB! Dad's calling you!" Mrs. Chesney leaned out of the window, waving a yellow duster to attract her son's attention. Rob was just off on his bicycle to spend a pleasant morning at the swimming baths.

"What's Dad want?"

"Come back, Rob. He's had a letter and it's about you."

Rob dismounted and propped his bicycle against the front gate.

"I haven't done anything, Mum. What's up?"

"It's what you are going to do. Come and hear the letter."

Mr. Chesney had got up late that morning. Being in a hurry he had cut himself while shaving and he was further delayed by the letter which he had read while consuming his breakfast of cornflakes and sausages.

"Hey, Rob! Here's a go! Your Uncle Joseph has written . . ."

"Step-uncle," interrupted Grandma, a determined old lady with a mind of her own despite

2

her delicate health. "Joseph Chesney is no son of mine . . . my step-son and a rogue at that!"

"Now come, Mother," said Mr. Chesney. "Joseph is my half-brother and we have always been good friends."

"When he remembered your existence," said Grandma tartly. "He took more than his fair share of your dad's money."

"The money came from his mother originally, so Dad's will was fair enough . . ."

"What's all that got to do with me?" demanded Robin, who was aching to join his pals at the baths, for the weather was hot. It was mid-August, the summer holidays and no time for discussing bygone family rows about wills.

"Your uncle has written urging me to go immediately to stay with him at his week-end cottage in Scotland. He does not say why, but I expect he just wants company . . . perhaps someone to help a bit while he is writing his books. He is not ill or anything. Of course I cannot possibly go. There's my work to consider and I am anxious to get the garden in order. The landlord's a bit crusty about the weeds. I hate gardening but the house does not belong to me so I cannot put down concrete."

"Vandal!" said Grandma. "Concrete indeed!"

Rob edged towards the door.

"So you won't be able to go then?"

"No, but you will. Your uncle has sent the money for your railway fare and he mentions that my son will do instead if I cannot come. You will have to go tonight."

"Me? But I don't know Uncle Joseph and there's a football match I want to see this afternoon too."

"You can go to the match first, then catch the train at 6.14. Mum will pack up your things and I will see you off. Don't worry about your uncle. He is a good sort, bit of a bookworm, history and all that. Lives in the Middle Ages, an eccentric, old Joseph."

"Eccentric my foot! He's crackers!" said Grandma in her gruff old voice.

Robin's mother began to look alarmed. "Is it safe for Rob to go such a long journey to stay with someone like Joseph?"

"Robin likes long journeys," said Grandma acidly. "He doesn't even mind visiting red-hot Communists!"

Mr. Chesney hurried off to his work, calling reassuring remarks to his wife. Joseph wouldn't hurt a fly, though being a bit absent-minded he might forget the fly's existence. Joseph was not one for writing letters.

So Robin cycled off to the swimming-baths and his father to the works.

"Do the boy good," said Mr. Chesney to himself as he went. "A journey to Scotland will encourage independence without any tomfoolery like going off to Russia on his own. Holiday for the lad! I can fix up someone to meet him in Edinburgh. Ferguson has a son there. Good chap, Ferguson."

Mr. Chesney had not forgotten the Patagonian affair, but he was tactful enough not to mention it to his son. Robin however was to be reminded again of that adventure even that very day. His desire to watch the Friendly between Norwich and Colchester had an unexpected result.

Robin and his gang were all booing their heads off about an unpopular decision on the part of the referee when a large and sticky doughnut came hurtling into the crowd of them and hit Robin smack in the face.

In these days bricks, bombs, stones and C.S. gas get tossed around fairly frequently, but a doughnut as a missile is not often used. Robin immediately sprang to his feet, fists clenched, looking out for the American who had thrown it. Americans are not usually football fans, being more addicted to baseball, but East Anglia sees a good many of that nationality knocking around,

and, as the Yanks invented the doughnut, as well
as being the first to drop litter on the moon, it
was natural to expect that the doughnut had
come from one of them.

But there were none at the match. Instead, as
he glared through a mist of jam, sugar and
grease, Robin Chesney saw that his attacker was
no other than his one-time partner in crime, the
long-faced, bespectacled Howard Hunt, sitting
just two rows away.

"Hi Rob!" said Hunt in a voice that seemed
to boom above the uproar of the crowd. "What
about another little journey together?"

Wiping off doughnut remains with the back of
his still clenched fist, Robin scrambled over the
legs of his companions and approached his former
friend.

"You shut your trap, How. If you let those
chaps know about you know what, I'll strangle
you."

"Take it easy," growled Hunt. "No offence
meant. I could not attract your attention any
other way and I wanted to talk to you. We were
friends once, you know."

"That's all over," said Robin savagely. "D'you
mean you've come to live here?"

"I'm staying with my Aunt Susan at Sprowston. She has a bungalow there and she works in

Norwich. My folk have gone to an educational conference in Sweden. It's deadly in Sprowston. I'm glad I met you. We can get around together."

Howard's people had taken that old affair very seriously. No spanking and then forget it for him. No little wry hints like Grandma's. In Howard's case, his misbehaviour had been discussed and discussed. His parents had said a lot and they went on saying it. Robin had never heard of Aunt Susan, but if she talked as much as Mr. and Mrs. Hunt, the whole of Sprowston, Norwich and Norfolk would have found out about Patagonia and Russia before long. Aunt Susan must be prevented somehow from blabbing out the wretched tale. She must not know that the Chesneys lived in Norwich or that Howard and Robin had ever set off on that ridiculous adventure. Once Howard had safely returned to his educational parents, the secret was fairly safe. Old ladies (and aunts are generally aged) have other things to gossip about more interesting to them than the mistakes of schoolboys unknown.

Howard Hunt must be persuaded to keep his mouth shut while staying in Sprowston.

"Let's clear out of this. We can talk better away from all this row." A thunderous uproar applauding Norwich's first goal drowned the suggestion, but Howard got the idea and they left the football ground. It was maddening to have to lose the rest of the game, but Howard must not meet Robin's gang on any account.

They went some distance from Carrow Road before Robin got a word in. Howard was busy describing the mortifying experiences he had gone through when his parents changed their teaching posts and went to Bristol.

"I thought the ragging would stop in a new place," he grumbled. "But no! My mother told the headmaster of my new school all about us going off like that. She said he ought to know if he was to understand my psychological make-up, and the blighter told the rest of the staff. I had not been at the school for two days before the Geography master asked me to describe my journey to Russia to the whole group. They winkled the story out of me right away. Ever since then someone is always pulling my leg and jeering. I've had a mouldy life."

"We were daft then, but the point is that we are not kids now. We've got to live it down and we shall never do that if people keep on raking up the past. Tell you something, How, you simply must keep your mouth shut about us going off to Russia. So far nobody in Norwich has connected me with that affair. Nobody knows except my old grandma and she is ill most of the time and she doesn't make friends with the people here, because she is too old to be bothered. So don't go telling your aunt. Old ladies always gossip."

Howard looked disappointed. "My aunt isn't as old as your grandma. I wanted to ask you to tea. She's quite decent really. We could be friends again. It's deadly being on one's own."

Robin shook his head.

"Sorry, How, but I shan't be here. I'm off to Scotland tonight . . . going to stay with an old half-uncle in East Lothian. I don't know him at all. Dad likes him but my grandma can't bear him. She was his stepmother and he didn't like her."

"Just my luck," groaned Howard, "you going away when I'm here. It's bad enough to be parked with an aunt who is cross because she is longing to go to Scotland herself and can't because of me. Life is downright hard."

"Sorry," said Rob, though he did not feel sorry. He was quite sure that a renewed friendship with Howard Hunt would bring complications. He was glad to be going to Scotland.

Howard peered through his large glasses and spoke wistfully.

"I promise word of honour that I won't tell anyone about us going to Russia. May I come with you when you go to . . .?"

"No. Certainly not."

"Aunt Susan wants to join a party of friends on the Isle of Skye. She'd drive us all the way to Scotland. That would save you the railway fare."

Not for a million pounds would Robin mix himself up in another journey with Howard.

"Skye is not anywhere near East Lothian, and my uncle has sent the railway fare. It's all fixed up about my journey too. Someone is needed to help Uncle Joseph, so you would be in the way."

Howard was extremely disappointed, but he was not going to be snubbed. He demanded the address in Scotland so that he could write a letter. Robin was not too keen on giving the information and he hated writing letters himself, but he had found out a few particulars about his uncle when the session at the swimming baths was over. He thought it wiser not to make an enemy of Howard, there was no need to answer letters—so he tore out a page from his diary and scrawled:
Blackbrae, Innernuik, by Haddington, East Lothian, Scotland.

"It's a very remote place," he said, "right away in the Lammermuir Hills, just about as far from Skye as from Norwich, I should think."

He hoped the distance would be off-putting,

and to discourage Howard even more he added in a tone by no means cordial:

"My half-uncle is most peculiar. Dad says he is a good sort, but you should hear Grandma on him! She says he wangled Grandfather's money and she and my dad were left very badly off. So don't you think of coming. He might be vexed."

"The Lammermuir Hills must be interesting. I've read Sir Walter Scott's *Bride of Lammermuir*. I'll send it to you . . . and *The Heart of Midlothian* too. Scott is very thrilling if you like a bit of history."

"I don't," said Robin hastily. "Please don't trouble. I have to help my uncle and may not have time for reading. Well, goodbye old chap. Keep that journey of ours under your hat . . . Ta-ta!"

He cycled off home, feeling an awful ass, but quite relieved that he had seen the last of his old pal. If Howard Hunt spilt the beans about the Patagonian Affair, well, that would be too bad. He had been warned.

Howard Hunt stood still in the road staring gloomily at the disappearing figure. A bus drew up at the stopping place nearby and a boy sprang off.

Howard was too much engrossed with his own disappointment to notice the bus passenger. The boy noticed him, however, and clapped him on the shoulder with a cheery "Hi, How!"

For a moment Howard's short-sighted eyes gaped through the thick lenses. His mouth dropped open.

"Well what a coincidence!" he stuttered. "Both of you in one day! And I never thought I'd see you or Rob Chesney again!"

"It's a coincidence that I see you. I was expecting to see Rob though. I've come on purpose to see him. The woman who lived next door to the Chesneys in Tooting gave me his address in Norwich. I've been on the Broads with my cousins and I came in to Norwich today specially to see Rob. And now I can take both of you at once!"

"What for? You didn't do us much good, did you? You and your treasure map! Rob Chesney doesn't want to have anything more to do with you or with me, and he's going to Scotland by the night train, so he won't be pleased if you turn up on a visit today."

Tom Hopkins kicked the edge of the kerb with the toe of his shoe. His eyes were thoughtful.

"Going to Scotland, is he? Grouse-shooting perhaps? Which part of Scotland?"

"I'm not telling you. He doesn't want ever to hear about you and your treasure map again."

"I've got a better treasure to tell him and you about, Howard. That's why I wanted to meet you again."

"I do not want to hear anything about any treasure of yours," said Howard with great dignity, "and I cannot waste time talking to you. My parents would be much displeased if they knew that we had met. They do not approve of you."

Tom Hopkins grinned. The disapproval of Mr. and Mrs. Hunt did not seem to worry him.

"I'm going home tomorrow, so I have only this one chance of meeting either of you in Norwich. Can you give me Rob's address in Scotland? I might write—"

"You are not going to have either of our addresses."

"Places in Scotland have such odd names, Auchterlochtie, Crianlarich and Achnashellach . . . I don't suppose you could even pronounce the name of Rob's address, much less spell it."

Howard fell into the trap easily as Tom knew he would.

"Of course I can spell it, and pronounce it too. It's simple enough, Blackbrae, Innernuik by Haddington. But you won't remember it."

Tom laughed. He had a good memory.

"Well, so long, Howard. I won't keep you if

your parents wouldn't wish us to be friends any more. I'm sorry about that map. Someday I must tell you of a better treasure—"

He did not finish his remark, for Howard had stalked off. Howard was annoyed three times over. He had lost the end of the match, which was something to do, though he was not a football fan. Rob Chesney had not wanted to talk to him and was going to Scotland. Lucky dog! And Tom Hopkins had turned up again and had got the better of him once more. Tom could not possibly remember an address like that without writing it down . . . or could he? Tom was pretty clever three years ago. Rob would be mad if he found out that Howard had betrayed him to their enemy, Thomas Hopkins.

Bah! Everything was mouldy!

On the whole, though, not quite so dusty. He might go down to the railway station and do a bit of engine-spotting, and he could look up the trains to Scotland. No harm to see Rob off. Aunt Susan was not expecting him back to tea. He could get a cuppa at the station.

Chapter 3

I'LL TAK' THE HIGH ROAD

THE Chesney family did their best to give Robin a good send-off. His mother packed his clothes and a good supply of eatables in case he should be hungry on the long journey. His father gave him five pounds, cautioning him to spend it with care and adding some advice about doing all in his power to help Uncle Joseph, a proud man who would never have asked for help unless he was in real need. Grandma peered at her grandson through faded but still twinkly eyes, and said hoarsely:

"Don't give my love to my stepson. He won't want it. Don't mention me or you'll be in trouble. Ha ha! If you are going to stay with your Uncle Joseph, Robin my lad, just you keep your wits about you. You haven't much between your ears. Make the best of what you have!"

Rob's father escorted him to the station, found him a corner seat and said goodbye rather quickly, as he wanted to get ahead with his gardening.

"Thanks a lot, son, for taking my place. Your uncle is not so bad as Grandma makes out. He's eccentric, a bit of a bookworm. Don't forget to change at Peterborough. I've arranged with Ferguson at the works for his son to meet you at Edinburgh. You remember Frank Ferguson? He got into Edinburgh University. His dad rang him up and he will be meeting you first thing tomorrow morning, soon after four. You pay for his breakfast and he will drive you out to Innernuik, so you will be there in good time."

Mr. Chesney waved goodbye and hurried off to his gardening. His place at the door was immediately taken by Howard Hunt who had been lurking in the background in the hopes of getting in a word with Rob.

"I guessed you'd travel by this train," he panted. "I dashed back to the bungalow to get those books but Aunt Susan hadn't got either of them. She doesn't read at all. I will send you *The Bride of Lammermuir* as soon as I go home."

"Please don't. I'm not gone on Scott myself. I hope you will enjoy your visit to Norwich. Norwich is a fine city. Ask your aunt to take you to see the Cathedral and the Castle. The Wild Life Park is not far off and the Broads . . ." Rob's voice trailed away. He could see that Howard was not going to be impressed with the beauties of Norfolk and her chief city. His heart was in Scotland and his woebegone expression revealed utter dejection.

"You don't know my aunt. She does not want to be bothered with me. There's a lot I could have told you if your dad hadn't talked for such a long time . . ."

He jerked away from the door and stood mournfully waving as the train moved out of the station.

As far as Robin knew, the journey was uneventful. He got outside most of his mother's supply of food and read his football paper before changing at Peterborough so there was not much to do after that and he went to sleep. The most important incident happened while he was, as the saying goes "in the arms of Morpheus". A sharp-faced middle-aged man who sat opposite yawned and leaned back, ready also for a bit of kip. When raising his eyes, he caught sight of the modest suitcase which Robin's mother had so carefully packed for him.

The man frowned. He looked round at the other passengers in the long coach. Most of them were asleep or nodding over books or newspapers. The man stood up and carefully read the label Mrs Chesney had written. He studied the sleeping boy in the seat opposite, then quietly took down the case and opened it. One by one he took out shirts, socks, sponge-bag, bathing trunks, pyjamas and handkerchiefs. He looked into the package containing the remains of sandwiches, crumbs of fruit cake and half a bar of chocolate. He noted the writing-paper and stamped addressed envelope put in to remind Robin to write home. What he expected to find in a schoolboy's luggage was not evident. There were certainly no uncut diamonds or microfilms hidden there. The man copied out the address of Robin's home but not that of his destination, which he probably knew already. Then he restored the re-packed suitcase to its position on the rack and leaned back in his seat, deep in thought.

The inquisitive stranger had changed his seat before Robin woke up. He did not speak to the boy, but waited until he had witnessed the meeting between Robin and a very typical young student who greeted the lad with a hearty, "Hi chum! D'you remember me? I'm Frank Ferguson from Norwich and my dad's a mate of yours. What about a spot of breakfast before we drive to Haddington?"

It was still dark when they breakfasted in a transport café known to young Ferguson and they sat for a while talking.

"It's no earthly use waking your uncle at crack of dawn," said Ferguson. "If this is your first

visit to Edinburgh, you ought to see something
of the Royal City. What about climbing up to
the Castle at sunrise and doing the Royal Mile,
and you simply must see the Forth Bridge and
Holyrood House:

> 'that noble stately dome
> Where Scotia's kings of other years,
> Famed heroes! had their royal home.'

as your namesake, Robbie Burns, so aptly put it."

They went sight-seeing in the misty dawn, and
even with such an early start there was not time
to see everything. They had to have a look at the
shops which sold tartans of all the clans, Ferguson
proudly pointing out his own green and blue
plaid, and the souvenir shops where Cairngorm
brooches, thistle tie-pins and Scottish shortbread
abounded.

It was after one o'clock when Rob remembered
his father's injunction to arrive in good time at
Blackbrae. So they set off to Ferguson's digs
where he kept his motor bicycle and then fared
forth towards Haddington.

Ferguson did not know the remoter parts of
East Lothian particularly well and he had mis-
taken Robin's pronunciation of Innernuik for
Innerwick which is a small place near the coast.
His mistake took them considerably out of the

way, though they had a lovely drive along the coast road through Portobello, Musselburgh, Prestonpans and Dunbar. The scenery of the Firth of Forth with the Bass Rock and all that caused them to stop several times and naturally they had to get refreshment occasionally. The Lammermuir Hills stood out blue in the distance but did not seem to get any nearer. They arrived at the grey old town of Haddington and were directed back to the coast. Ferguson was sure that his road-sense was infallible, yet nobody at Innerwick had ever heard of Blackbrae or Mr. Joseph Chesney.

It was late afternoon when they finally arrived at the cluster of small stone cottages high among the hills which formed the hamlet of Innernuik. Ferguson drew up by a telephone kiosk where an old woman was taking in her washing from a line in her garden.

"Blackbrae is it ye're wishing? Och aye! It's a wee way from here up the brae and doon the lane on the left. Blackbrae stands a bit doonhill on the far side." She peered at Ferguson and her eyes travelled over the passenger on the pillion.

"It's that boy again," she said. "Mr. Chesney was saying when he came to use the telephone that he'd been back. . . . He's been coming back these thirty years."

She tossed her clean sheets back into the basket and carried them into her cottage.

"Up the brae and down the lane on the left. Do you think you could walk the last bit, Rob? We've run things a bit late and I've a date with a lassie for this evening, so, I ought to be getting back," said Ferguson.

He buzzed off and Robin climbed the hill with his small case, wondering as he went what the old woman had meant about a boy coming back for thirty years. Then he forgot all about the mysterious boy and began to enjoy the wide sweep of the hills and the clear air with its faint tang of the sea.

Just over the brow of the hill there was a turning into a rutted lane, down which he could see a square stone house with a slate roof and a chimney on each end like two pointed ears. The walled garden held a few shrubs, many weeds and one pine tree rather too close to the house. It looked a good tree for climbing. At the back there were some farm buildings and before the gate stood a car beside which an elderly man was pacing up and down in a state of great agitation. He was constantly looking at his watch as if pressed for time. Catching sight of Rob, the man blazed forth in fury;

"Get out! Go away at once!"

Robin hesitated. He did not appreciate a welcome of this kind.

"I am Robin Chesney," he said. "I have come to stay with my uncle, Mr. Joseph Chesney."

The man's face went red with rage. "Don't tell me lies, boy. Clear out, I say. I am Joseph Chesney and the nephew whom I am expecting is a grown man. Boys, boys, boys, always up to mischief!"

Robin did not clear out. He held his ground.

"My dad is Richard Chesney, your half-brother. He sent me because he could not take a holiday from the works just yet and he had to do some gardening. I can be quite helpful. Mum says I am handy in the house."

Mr. Joseph Chesney puffed and then suddenly calmed down.

"I am not looking for a housemaid, boy. Yes, you are like Richard only your hair is too long! You have a look of him, but you are too young. Richard was married nearly twenty years ago. Stephen should be eighteen at least."

"Stephen died when he was a baby, long before I was born. Mum talks about him sometimes. She has some photos of him. I'm the only other son."

Uncle Joseph grunted, his heavy brows drawn in a close frown as he scrutinized the boy. He looked at his watch.

"If you travelled by the night train, you should have arrived hours ago. I told Richard to take a taxi from Edinburgh. I have to catch the late flight to Belfast and there is no time to explain everything to you. Much too young . . . what's the use of sending a boy . . . as if I have not had worry enough with boys. Well, I suppose I must make the best of what I've got.

"Listen, boy. Are you nervous about sleeping alone in the house? No? I must leave immediately. There's a cottage down the lane. The good woman does my cleaning and cooking. Comes in twice a week. She will be in tomorrow. Meanwhile go down the hill and telephone to your father. Explain that I have to be away on important business and he must come or send someone responsible. I cannot leave this place empty even for one night. You have come so late and I have no time to explain. Here's the key. Keep the doors locked and the shutters closed.

"There's plenty of food in the larder. Don't let that boy into the house, or any boys, for you don't know who I am talking about. Most important. No boys. . . ."

In much agitation, Uncle Joseph sprang into his car, drew out the clutch and drove off.

Chapter 4

LANDED PROPRIETOR

"TALK about Uncle Joseph being a rum 'un! He's bonkers! What do I do next? I'm not going all the way back to that telephone before I've had a cup of tea. Not me!"

The car had lurched up the rutted lane and swerved into the road in a cloud of dust. Robin was left alone before a bleak-looking house surrounded by purple heather and rolling hills. There wasn't a soul in sight. He could not even see the cottage which his uncle had mentioned.

It would have been wise to do as he had been told and make for the telephone at once. He knew that Mum would not dream of allowing her son to stay alone in a remote spot like Blackbrae, but if Dad couldn't come, who else would? Most people are away on holiday in the middle of August.

"I'll have a look-round first and see what's needed."

He dumped his suitcase in the dark, narrow hall and set off to explore Blackbrae. Uncle Joseph, Dad had said, owned a house in the suburbs of Newcastle, so he really had no need for a weekend cottage. Robin's first impression was that this was a dumping-ground for his uncle's unwanted lumber.

Chiefly books. A bit of a bookworm, was he? Dad's words were an understatement. The cottage was crammed with books. In the dark hall Robin knocked over a pile of them groping his way to find the light switch. There was no light switch because there was no electric light. He opened the sitting-room door and faced a tall bookcase full of books, a half-opened wooden crate filled with aged and rather dirty tomes, books on the piano, books piled on the floor, on the old-fashioned leather sofa and on the chairs. They were all old books such as one might find in a cheap remnant box outside a second-hand shop, and they smelt fusty because all the downstairs windows were closed and shuttered.

In the kitchen more books were scattered among the cups on the oak dresser, in the scullery among the pots and pans.

"Like living in a library," muttered Robin. "I shall turn into a book myself before long."

The fire had gone out in the old-fashioned kitchen range and there was neither electricity nor gas to boil a kettle on. He discovered an ancient oil stove which he managed to light with difficulty and much smoke. Water had to be pro-

cured from a pump in the scullery. Robin's city
life had not prepared him for such primitive
conditions.

He enjoyed his tea though, in spite of its sooty
flavour. The home-made bread and the country
butter were delicious, and he felt a new man after
his meal.

"I will explore a bit before going to the telephone. Mum will want to hear all about it," he
decided.

He did not bother to visit the bedrooms. "They
are always the same in every house." The garden
was wild and a mass of weeds everywhere except
in one patch where Uncle Joseph had presumably
made a half-hearted attempt to plant cabbages.
He had raked over the ground and inserted some
weary plants which he had forgotten to water.
Like Dad, Uncle Joseph was not a gardener at
heart. Robin thought he might himself have a go
at it if his visit to Blackbrae lasted long enough.

The farm buildings stood rather too near the
back of the house. Once long ago the previous
owners of Blackbrae had kept horses and cows,
pigs and hens. No factory farming in those days.
The hens must have had free range over garden
and moorland. Uncle Joseph ought to give up his
books and start the farm going again, decided
Robin.

Blackbrae was a mixture, positively prehistoric as regards amenities, grim and forbidding to look at, yet not without charm. Yes, the view was quite fabulous, the rolling hills all blue far away and splashed with purple heather and bracken tipped with gold near the house. He liked the scream of the sea-gulls flying in from the coast, the scarlet berries of the shrubby rowan trees in the garden and the call of a grouse in the undergrowth. He did not know it to be a grouse, but he connected grouse with Scotland, and he had never heard before that low "Ow . . . Ow . . ." followed by a rapid "Kowk-ok-ok-ok-ok".

He took a turn round the place and felt decidedly pleased with himself. He had always lived in a city, so this was a novel experience. He felt he was now a landed proprietor, with an estate of his own, for the time being anyway. He saw himself huntin', shootin', fishin', and dis-cussing the weather and the crops with other landowners.

A grand time he would have, doing as he pleased, eating when and what he liked, going to bed only when tired. There'd be no need to bother about washing, for that meant pumping and heating bath-water.

He descended from his high estate with a bump, for doing without washing reminded him of the horrible hiding-place in the hold of that ghastly ship. The memory still recurred, though it no longer gave him nightmares. He'd made a fool of himself trying to live on his own (you couldn't quite count Howard Hunt as a real person). He would not do that again, not till he was eighteen and grown up. He carefully locked the front door and set off to find the telephone.

His mother answered the call. She was jittery with anxiety.

"Rob darling is that you? You've arrived all right then. Take care of yourself, dear. I can't stop now. I'm expecting the doctor . . ."

"Is Grandma worse, Mum?"

"She's very bad, but it's not Grandma this time. It's Dad. He fell over the rake, in the garden—yes dear, the rake. He thinks his leg is broken. There's the doctor at the door. Goodbye darling, I must fly. Take care of yourself. . . ."

She rang off.

Robin whistled. If he had rung up at once as Uncle Joseph said, Dad would not have been in the garden. He would have been packing his bag to come to Blackbrae, or ringing up his boss to arrange about the work, or even frantically trying to get someone else to take his place with his son in Scotland. Now poor old Dad had a broken leg and Mum was rushed off her feet with two invalids, and Dad could be as difficult as Grandma when he was ill. No use worrying Mum any more.

"I could talk to the woman who does the cleaning tomorrow," he thought. "But I'll be all right alone for tonight."

The old lady from the cottage by the telephone came out for a chat. She liked to keep up with whatever was going on. She clucked like a hen when she heard what had happened.

"I shouldn't care to sleep alone at Blackbrae myself," she said. "He might come back."

"Who might come back?"

"I'll say no more. It's not for me to frighten a lad like you. But mind you lock the doors."

Robin wondered what the tale was she had begun before. Some nonsense about a sort of Peter Pan who never grew up in thirty years. Country folk, he thought, still believe in fairies. A simple old woman, that's all. I'm not scared of sleeping alone in a house. Robinson Crusoe was a lot worse off than I am. I have a place to live in, plenty of food in the larder and enough books to last a lifetime. The lack of both television and radio do not matter. One can do without them in the summer.

He went into the kitchen and stood staring, puzzled.

When he had his tea, he had swept all the books off the table. He was quite sure of that. He had eaten plenty of bread and butter and honey, but he certainly had not finished the loaf, or scraped the honey-pot. Nor had he added his cup and plate to the pile of unwashed dishes which Uncle Joseph had left in the sink. Was he becoming absent-minded and forgetful, or turning into an eccentric like his uncle?

He glanced at the book lying where his plate had been. It was a child's picture-book, *Goldilocks*, a tale he remembered from his primary school days, the story of some stupid girl who blundered into a house belonging to three bears. He hurled the grubby picture-book across the room and picked a more serious volume . . . and dropped it, as if it had been red hot. The book was open, and the first words he saw were those of a couplet he had heard many times in West Tooting Comprehensive School;

"Westward ho! with a rumbelow,
And hurra for the Spanish Main, O!"

Uncle Joseph had not put that book on the table. Robin knew that for a fact. Probably seeing Howard Hunt the day before had re-awakened the memory of that wretched trip to South America and had somehow induced Robin to select *West-Ward Ho* out of all the hundreds of books in Blackbrae, though he had no recollection of putting any book on the table, or of removing his tea-things.

He boiled a kettleful of water and washed the dishes. He stacked as many books as possible into a large laundry basket and that was as much house-work as he could face for the first evening. So he took a walk round the premises to cheer himself up. The sun was setting by that time and sending a sort of amber glow over the hills which turned the trunk of the pine tree quite red and made the windows glitter. He surveyed the scenery, wondering how Dad was getting on with a broken leg.

Somebody giggled. A voice whispered. He heard the words though he saw no one.

"What an ass! It's a fabulous idea!"

The annoying thing about a whisper is that it might come from anybody. A voice is easy to recognize, but the whisperer might be male or female, old or young, or indeed nobody at all. Trees whisper in the wind; a stream whispers as it chuckles over pebbles; newspapers whisper when the reader turns a page. But such whispers do not utter words. The speaker must be quite near for the words were heard.

But there was nobody in the lane, nobody on the stretch of heather in front of the house, nobody in the garden. On the left side of the

house, the path led round to the outhouses, the
stable and the barn, passing Uncle Joseph's cabbage patch. The hill sloped down steeply on the
right side and a stream gushed out of the rock and
trickled off behind the farm buildings. Anybody
whispering round there could not be heard from
the front, yet only the house offered any place for
concealment and Blackbrae was strongly built.
Those stone walls would be sound-proof against a
brass band!

He went indoors, feeling slightly ridiculous.

"I'm imagining things," he muttered as he set
about preparing some supper, scrambled egg on
one of those big flat rolls and a mug of cold milk.
Fortunately Uncle Joseph had a good store of
apples.

Before scrambling his eggs, however, he decided
that he had better inspect the upper floor, just
in case any whisperer should be lurking there. He
found some candles and went upstairs.

Like the home of the Three Bears, Blackbrae
had three bedrooms, a big one, with Uncle
Joseph's unmade bed, a middle-sized one, made
ready for his nephew, and a small one which
Robin had already seen from the hay-loft. All
three were plentifully supplied with books, mostly
very old and dull. Nowhere did he see any sign of
the whisperer, so he chose the most readable of

the books, *The Cock House at Fellsgarth* by Talbot Baines Reed, and John Buchan's *The Thirty-Nine Steps*. Though not exactly trendy, these two were more modern than most of Uncle Joseph's strange collection. He took his supper to bed and settled down to a good read.

Travelling all night and sight-seeing all day made him sleepy, and after half an hour the two books slithered off the bed with a clatter. He was just enough awake to blow out the candle and then he fell asleep completely. The moon was shining into his window when he shot suddenly out of bed, startled by the noise of not two but about fifty books crashing down the staircase, followed by a distinct chuckle.

Someone had stumbled into the pile of books which Uncle Joseph had left on the landing.

This was the moment for a deed of heroism. The gallant householder should have seized the poker and rushed out to tackle the intruder. Robin did neither. He was half asleep, bewildered by the strangeness of his room and the unexpected noise, and downright scared by the weird chuckle after that objectionable whispering in the garden.

Reason deserted him. Common sense failed. Without pausing to think twice, he threw open the door of the big wardrobe and scrambled inside. Uncle Joseph had left some of his clothes there, and they smelt horribly of mothballs. He was afraid of being suffocated, but even more afraid of the thing that whispered and chuckled in Blackbrae.

Chapter 5

MR. CHESNEY'S HOBBY

ANYONE can be brave when surrounded by admiring companions. Courage at midday burns like a flaming torch, but you just try to be valiant when shut up alone in a fusty wardrobe in a strange and melancholy house entirely remote from any other living creature! See if your courage does not vanish like a snuffed-out candle flame!

Through the keyhole, Robin could see a streak of moonlight. The bedroom windows had curtains but no shutters and the keyhole was too small to reveal any more than that one stray beam. He thought he heard soft movements in the big bedroom next door, and presently the sound of a car in the lane, drawing up and then driving away again. After that there was no sound in the house but the monotonous ticking of the hall clock, a big grandfather type.

When morning came he emerged, stiff, cold and much ashamed of himself. Nobody, he determined, would ever know how he had spent that first night at Blackbrae. He had an early breakfast and then made a complete inspection of the whole house. The sun shone. The oil stove worked better, and a good breakfast restored him to his normal self.

Downstairs all was in order. The doors were locked and the shutters closed. The books had tumbled from the top of the landing to the hall floor and he wondered whether after all the midnight intruder was only a stray cat or even a rat who had knocked over the untidy pile. In the big bedroom however he noticed that the window could be opened easily by anybody who had climbed up the pine tree. A cat could get out that way, but a cat would not close the window after her when departing. It is a tricky business pushing up a window when both cords have gone and to climb through means risking a broken spine, for Blackbrae window frames were old and very strong. Somebody might have entered the house that way while Robin was out telephoning, somebody who whispered and giggled. Perhaps there were two intruders, one holding up the window and the other in the upper branches of the pine tree. Robin had looked round the garden and the lane. He had not thought of looking up.

A burglar by day is not so alarming as a burglar by night. That window must be fastened and then no more need to worry.

He was hunting for a hammer and nails in the scullery when a sharp squeal made him turn to the back door. Before it stood a small girl clutching a milk can and trembling like an aspen leaf, her face white and her eyes round with terror. She stared at Robin as if he were a snake.

"What's up? Don't scream like that or you'll break my eardrums. What d'you want? Are you the milkman?"

Milkmaid would have been a better description, but this was no time for nice distinctions. He only wanted to cheer up the poor kid.

Colour stole back into her cheeks. She nodded. "I brings the milk for Mr. Chesney," she said. "Hae ye come back again then?"

"I never was here before. Mr. Chesney's my uncle. I'm staying while he's away."

"You're real then, not a ghostie?"

"Course I'm real. There's no such thing as ghosts."

"Morag at the school tellt me that the ghost-boy comes to Blackbrae at night. I thocht you was maybe him. Will you gie me the milk-can back, please?"

He tipped the milk into a jug and returned the can. Ghost indeed! Nonsense! Nobody believes in ghosts when the sun is shining. He almost laughed as he saw the child running down the lane and peeping back over her shoulder as if ghoulies and ghosties and long-legged beasties were chasing her.

What was it the woman by the telephone had said? "I shouldn't care to sleep alone at Blackbrae myself. . . . He might come back. . . ."

Rubbish! He gave up the notion of fastening the window. He did not wish anyone to think he was scared. Instead, he would go fishing. There was some fishing tackle under the stairs and a box of beautifully made flies in the kitchen drawer. He might as well have a try at fly-fishing.

He returned in the afternoon, his creel empty, for he had not come across any sizeable piece of water, though he had wandered far and lost himself several times. He was hungry and hot and his temper was not improved by the sight of a perambulator with a baby in it parked in the garden of Blackbrae. The front door was wide open as were all the windows, with shutters thrown back and the sunlight pouring into the dreary rooms. A buxom young woman was singing in the kitchen as she rolled out pastry on a floured board. She smiled when she saw him.

"You'll be Mr. Chesney's nephew then. He was expecting a grown man. My wee Jeannie that brought the milk was scairt when she saw a laddie instead. It is Mrs. MacTaggart I am and I come twice a week to do for the old gentleman. I clean the house in the morning and bake for him afternoons."

She had made fresh bread with nutty golden crust, cake, scones and an apple pie as well as a small but juicy roast with vegetables from her garden.

"You will need a good supper after your walk," she said. "When do your parents arrive?"

She was shattered when she heard that Robin would be staying alone.

"I hope you will be all right," she said doubtfully. "Don't be listening to any tales about this house. There's been some boy playing round lately and annoying Mr. Chesney. The bairns at the school have made a mystery of it, but he's only a mischievous laddie. Mr. Chesney bought this house furniture and all, and there's nothing worth stealing here. No real burglar would waste his time on worm-eaten chairs and silver that's only plate and cheap at that. I'll get my husband to come up and mend the window cords this evening and you'll be quite safe if you keep the doors locked and the shutters up."

"What are all these books?" demanded Rob. "My dad said Uncle was a bookworm, but most of the books are kids' stuff or grubby old trash.

Is he going to set up a second-hand bookshop or what? He won't get many customers here."

Mrs. MacTaggart took the last jam tart out of the oven.

"He's a historian, Mr. Chesney. There's a big case full of history books in the parlour. They're his. The others, the old stuff, that's his kind nature. He bought up the contents of a dirty little shop in Edinbro because the owner was in trouble, sent to prison and wanted the money to help his family. The bookcase, that's Mr. Chesney's real hobby. The old books should be stored in cases, but he unpacked most of them and scattered them all over the place because of that boy I was telling you about. . . ."

The baby outside began to cry and she hurried out to comfort him, not without a few last words of encouragement for Robin.

"Don't you get thinking about ghosts now. I say to my Jeannie, put your trust in God in whose hands are the living and the dead. Folk have mixed up this young boy with another who used to live here many years ago and who went wrong. He was a bad one they say, but who are we to judge? We do not know whether he repented and was forgiven like the thief on the cross. That was long before I came to live here, more than twenty years, maybe thirty. This lad now is only a mischievous fellow, one of those vandals or hippies we hear of, skinheads or whatever they're called."

She went off down the lane to her cottage about a mile away, singing as she walked:

> "The Lord's my Shepherd, I'll not want
> He makes me down to lie,
> In pastures green He feedeth me
> The pleasant waters by."

Robin watched her departure with regret. Living alone was good enough in the morning sunshine, but a bit dreary in the evening. What did land-owners do without television when night came? Did they sit making up lists of fat stock or filling in income tax forms?

Hobbies, of course. Mrs. MacTaggart said Uncle Joseph's hobby was in the bookcase in the parlour. He lit the oil lamp, put up the shutters, though he forgot the kitchen window, and settled himself in the parlour, as Mrs. MacTaggart had called the sitting-room.

Uncle Joseph's hobby was history, not a subject dear to Robin's heart. In the glass case he had a lot of heavy tomes dealing with the period between William the Conqueror and Henry VII, a king chiefly remembered as being the father of Henry VIII, the king who had six wives. It was not a time that Robin knew well, though plentifully supplied with stirring events such as battles and beheadings. He opened one book, expecting to find tales of castles besieged, princes riding off to the wars, gallant deeds of high adventure. Instead he read without interest the fact that the word Escheat means "the lapsing of land to the Crown when the owner dies without heirs". He tried another lucky dip. This page was headed "Livery of Seisin". He did not trouble to read any more out of that book. A lawyer might want to read it of an evening, but not Robin Chesney.

Only one of his uncle's books was illustrated and that was concerned with heraldry. Robin's family sported no coats of arms, but he liked the clear vivid colours with their old names, or, argent, gules, azure, vert, sable, tenney and sanguine. It must have been quite thrilling making up a family crest: first a shield divided up into several parts: the Chief, the highest and most honourable; the Dexter, the right-hand side; the Sinister, the left-hand side; and the Base. There were the conventional figures, Pale, Bend, Fesse, Chevron, etc., and the Charges, the figures of animals, plants, instruments or imaginary monsters. A shield must have been a way of identifying people in the middle ages, and you'd need a flag or banner or shield when you were all encased in armour from head to foot.

A helmet now. The coat of arms ought to have a helmet on top of the escutcheon, full-faced with six bars for a king; sidelong with five bars for a duke; full-faced with vizor open for a knight; sidelong with vizor shut for an esquire.

How long ago it was, those far-off days when knights were bold and there were battles to fight and cities to conquer and treasures to seek. Of course, fighting was not all lions rampant and banners waving. After the battle, the shield would be bent and buckled and stained with blood, and even a gold helmet, full-faced with six bars, must have been uncomfortable, much worse than the crash-helmet Frank Ferguson had made Rob wear when riding from Edinburgh on his motor-cycle. Yet the esquire's steel helmet with vizor shut would be a help if you got a bash from a sword.

Shields, helmets, swords. Where had he heard something about that? Last time Mum took him to church, ages ago it was, the parson had talked about shields and swords and helmets. Yes, and the same bit of the Bible had turned up in an R.E. lesson at school soon after.

The Shield of Faith, wasn't it?

Mrs. MacTaggart had faith. She believed God would take care of her. The Helmet . . . that stood for Salvation, being saved from death and dishonour in the battle. The Sword. The Sword of

the Spirit which is the Word of God. How could
you use a Bible as a sword? Robin had never read
much of the Bible, snippets you learned at school;
going to Church with Mum occasionally, Harvest
Festivals, Christmas, Remembrance Sunday.

He looked round the book-filled parlour. There
was not one Bible among all these books.

He opened the front door and looked out. It
was raining now and the moon was hidden by
clouds.

"Coo! It's lonely!" He wrote a letter to his
mother, describing Uncle Joseph's booky house,
but saying nothing to worry her about his being
alone.

Only seven o'clock! Might as well have a
tinkle on the piano. He pushed the books off and
played "The Umbrella Man", "God Save the
Queen", and "Come Back to Erin", his whole
repertoire. The piano was out of tune and the
music, if music it could be called, echoed weirdly
through the empty house. He abandoned the
piano and returned to the kitchen, where Mrs.
MacTaggart's fire was blazing cheerfully. An old
volume of *Punch* for 1908 displaced from the piano
top might be amusing.

1908 seemed almost as remote as the distant
days of Medievalism. Wars and revolutions had
changed the world and its sense of humour.

At the corner of the road, a car turned down the lane. Its door slammed. The gate creaked and footsteps splashed through the puddles on the drive. Robin realized with alarm that he had not put up the kitchen shutters. Through the rain-spattered window stared a face, a long white face, its nose flattened against the glass, its large spectacles gleaming as they reflected the lamplight.

"Howard Hunt, you utter and absolute chump!"

This time Robin Chesney was downright glad to see the boy he had hoped never to meet again.

Chapter 6

REINFORCEMENTS

ROBIN threw open the front door. On the step stood a young woman in scarlet windcheater and slacks. She did not look a day over seventeen.

"She's my Aunt Susan," explained Howard in an apologetic manner. Robin stood staring. He had thought of Aunt Susan as exactly like Howard's mother, a school teacher every inch of her.

"May we come in? It's raining," suggested Howard. "My aunt wants to see your uncle."

Robin ushered them into the parlour which seemed a more suitable room than the kitchen. He shoved all the books off the horse-hair-covered couch, but the aunt did not sit down.

"My uncle is not at home," he admitted.

"That," said Aunt Susan with a bewitching smile, "is all to the good. Howard was mistaken in saying I wished to see your uncle. I do not. You may give him a message from me. I have driven my nephew all the way from Norwich so that he may come to your rescue."

Rescue indeed! The cheek of it! Howard Hunt to rescue anyone! Rescue from what?

"Howard told me that you are his best friend and that you have had to give up your holidays to help your poor old uncle, so I suggested that he should do the same and join you. Many hands make light work. Howard will give what help he can. He is very good at . . ." She paused, her eyes twinkled. "At washing the dishes. He could also arrange your books, and take the dog for a walk."

"I will be as useful as I can," said Howard mournfully.

"My uncle said I was not to have any more boys here. He specially mentioned that. The last thing he said was no boys."

Aunt Susan smiled graciously and swept out, her dark hair flopping over her eyes.

"Come to the car, Howard. I fear you are not wanted."

Howard followed her, the picture of dejection. Robin watched them from the doorstep, uncertain what to do. He would have welcomed any companionship at that moment, but Uncle Joseph might be annoyed if he came back and found an extra boy at Blackbrae.

Aunt Susan sprang lightly into her car, hurled a suitcase into a puddle by the gate, slammed the car door and backed up the lane, turned jerkily into the road and drove off.

Howard picked up his case and stumbled back to the house, shaking off the rain like a wet dog.

"It's not my fault," he said. "I only told her about you going to Scotland and she insisted that I was to come too. You see some of her friends had asked her to go and climb the mountains in Skye and they didn't ask me. She'd promised to look after me for the holidays, you see, before she heard about Skye and she was mad to go. I didn't tell her about going to Russia, because you said I wasn't to, and when she heard that my parents knew yours, she said it was perfectly safe for me to come. I hope you don't mind."

"Not particularly. But Uncle Joseph may be vexed."

"All right. I'll go and sleep in the fields. Nobody wants me. My mother and father have gone to an educational conference in Sweden. My aunt has gone to Skye. Nobody cares. I'll probably catch pneumonia with sleeping in the rain, or a cow may trample on me. That will be the end of me and nobody will be sorry."

"Cheer up, old horse! As a matter of fact, I'm quite glad to have someone to stay in this weird house. It is a bit spooky when you're alone. Let's get some supper."

Howard's melancholy vanished when he saw the results of Mrs. MacTaggart's excellent cooking. The lack of amenities in Blackbrae appalled him, for he had never even imagined life without modern comforts, life on dry land at least. Lamplight and candles, a cistern which had to be filled by a hand-pump, no central heating, no double glazing, electricity, gas, television, telephone, radio or fridge. This was a primitive existence, like living in the middle ages, he declared.

Mr. MacTaggart arrived at about nine and repaired the bedroom window. He seemed rather puzzled by the appearance of a second boy, for he knew of Mr. Chesney's annoyance about some lad who prowled round the place.

"I think he came last night," said Robin, "but I can't say for sure. It might have been a cat."

"There's been no cat at Blackbrae since Mr. Chesney was here. He hates cats worse than boys. Got an allergy to cats, he has. Mr. Chesney is a scholarly sort of man, one for books and old-fashioned ways."

With all precautions against burglars made, the house was secure against flesh and blood intruders. Wee Jeannie's ghosties did not worry Robin when he had someone to talk to. There was no disturbance that night.

The rain was over by morning and Howard was

thrilled by the view from the front of the house. The heather and the hills turned him all Scottish, and he raced downstairs singing:

"Scots wha hae wi' Wallace bled,
Scots whom Bruce has often led,
Welcome to your gory bed,
   Or to victorie!
Now's the day and now's the hour,
See the front of battle lour;
See approach proud Edward's power,
   chains and slaverie!"

"Come on laddie!" he shouted, in what he imagined to the language of the Scots, "come and tak' a wee dander. Stalk the deer and maybe put up a grouse or a brace of partridges. We have come to bonnie Scotland and so far I've not seen a kilt or a chieftain or a turretted castle, not a tartan or a clan. I'm for a bit of adventure!" Robin glowered at him.

"Don't talk to me about adventure. You and I have done enough adventuring. Your aunt brought you here to work and to make yourself useful to my uncle. We've got the supper things to wash as well as what we used for breakfast, and when that's done we shall do some gardening."

"August's the wrong time of year for gardening. It's too late for planting seeds."

5

"You can do some weeding. There's masses of weeds. Tell you what, How, let's dig up Uncle's cabbage patch at the side of the house. Uncle Joseph has had a go at it and he has planted some cabbages, but they are half dead. If we double dig that bit and water it well, we can re-plant the cabbages and have them growing by the time he comes back."

"Double-dig, that's heavy work," groaned Howard. "Didn't you say your dad fell over a spade? Gardening is unlucky in your family."

"It was a rake, not a spade. Yes, I know you would rather tidy up the books, but you are going to do a spot of hard labour in the open air this morning."

Howard's enthusiasm for Scotland waned. He sighed heavily. They dug all morning. First they removed the cabbages, then they dug all over the patch, tossing the earth aside until they had made a hole deep enough for a garden pool. Howard suggested that they ought to put in some manure and cover it with loose soil. But they had no manure and Robin's idea of double digging was to dig deep. They dug deep.

"I'm exhausted," said Howard.

"Press on regardless," urged Robin. "Ow! What's that?"

"It's a coffin," squealed Howard. "Your old

uncle has buried a body and decamped. You said he was a rogue."

"I never said it. He's not. Let's dig it out. We shall have to report this to the police."

"No. Bury it again and say nothing. My folks will be mad if I get into a mess with the police."

"I don't want to get Uncle Joseph into trouble either."

They squatted on the damp earth and studied the long, narrow box. It was made of stout wood and could not have been buried centuries ago, or the lid would have broken under their combined weights and spades. The box was too narrow to hold a full-grown man.

"It was not Uncle who buried it. The earth was only raked over at the top for those wilted cabbages. The ground had not been disturbed recently as deep as this. I wonder what's in it."

"I don't fancy opening a coffin," said Howard.

"Nor do I, it's a rotten thing to do, but this box is not big enough for a coffin. It might contain. . . ."

"Buried treasure!" Howard caught Robin's angry glare and added, "Or more books perhaps.'

"Let's feel how heavy it is."

They heaved it out and it was not any weight at all. The wood felt damp and musty. Robin took his spade and prised open the lid.

Inside the box was a neat lining of lead, on which reposed an old wooden pole, broken off at one end.

"Nothing but a stick! Who would want to bury a broomstick?"

"A witch perhaps. She may have used it to fly round on at night. She may even haunt Blackbrae with her ghost cat. Have you seen or heard anything spooky since you arrived, Rob?"

Robin ignored the question with dignity. He was not going to tell young Howard of that first night, spent in the wardrobe.

"The box is damp and musty outside, but the lining keeps the inside dry. I wonder if somebody long ago discovered valuables" (Robin generally avoided the use of the word "treasure") "and stole them, putting the old stick in their place."

"Might be. Let's shovel the earth back now. We have done enough double digging."

They put the box into its grave again and replaced the earth. The cabbages had got mixed up with the mud, so they had to be left to grow if they could. A good stamping reduced the plot to a semblance of order. Gardening was finished for the time.

"Let's collect some grub and explore the hills now," suggested Howard. "I'm sure there ought to be stags and Highland cattle knocking round."

Late in the afternoon they passed by the Mac-Taggarts' cottage on their way home. The good woman waved at them as they went by, but she did not speak for she was engaged in conversation with a middle-aged man who turned and stared at the two boys, giving them what Robin described as "a rather over-amiable grin".

The MacTaggart cottage was in a valley, some way beyond Blackbrae. To take a short cut, the boys crossed a stream and climbed a bracken-covered hill from the top of which they could look down on the house. They stood aghast. Blackbrae was no longer a desolate, lonely habitation. The stretch of heather before it was purple no longer. A gang of boys were busy pitching tents and digging trenches.

"It's Scouts!"

"Rot! Scouts know how to organize a camp. Those kids can't tell a tent-peg from a guy rope."

"It's Hippies come for a pop festival!"

"There aren't any girls in that camp. Pop groups always have more girls than blokes. Hi you there! Who are you and what are your lot doing here?"

"You there" was a small much-freckled lad.

"I'm Fred," he replied. "We are goin' to camp here."

"And who gave you permission, I'd like to know?"

Fred stared impudently and put out his tongue. "No business of yours. George, he brought us along."

"And who is George?"

"Him that took over the Youth Club two nights ago. He promised a free holiday to any of us who liked camping. I haven't got a tent, but I'm goin' to share. Are you campin' too? I ain't seen you before."

"We belong to the house over there," said Howard with importance.

"Ow! That's the Ghost's House, that is."

"Don't talk nonsense. There's no such thing as ghosts. Where is this George? Those boys ought not to be in my garden. They are trying to get into the house! Come on, How! We must drive them out. My uncle said, 'No boys in this house.' We must get rid of them."

"We are two against a score at least. We can't win."

"Well, step on the gas! Hurry!"

"I am hurrying," panted Howard.

Chapter 7

THE CAMP ON THE HEATHER

IN the camp somebody whistled. Immediately all the boys dropped tent-pegs and guy ropes and turned to stare at Robin and Howard as if two spacemen from a distant galaxy had dropped in for a visit to the planet Earth.

Then every boy in the camp laughed. Someone guffawed and the laughter spread like a ripple in a pond until the entire camp seemed to be yelling its head off.

The joke was incomprehensible to Robin and Howard. Why those guys should think it funny to see two more boys appearing on the horizon they could not understand. Also it was embarrassing to have to race through a crowd of giggling idiots and take possession of Uncle Joseph's property. They had more right to that stretch of heather than those rotten trespassers.

"Hey, you kids," bawled Robin as he drew near. "Clear out. This is private property. Take your camp somewhere else!"

"It's no your property," replied a sturdy lad.

"This land belongs to the Ghost and he's gi'en us permission to camp here."

"Look out for the bogey-man!" called another.

"Hobgoblins will catch you if you don't look out!"

"Who's afraid of the big bad wolf?"

"Hee hee hee! Ha ha ha!"

Robin pushed his way through the noisy campers with Howard at his heels, both of them putting on a "don't-care" manner though they did care. Ridicule is hard to bear.

The gate of Blackbrae was open and a tall boy carrying a bucket was disappearing in the direction of the spring. Two others were trying to force the lock of the front door. Robin disposed of them with the help of his fists. They ran off defeated, but still jeering. The boy with the bucket was not so easy to get rid of.

At first his manners were perfect. He stood still and listened to Robin's heated request for him to move on. His reply was quite without any of the raucous laughter uttered by the other campers.

"The campers need fresh drinking water. This spring is completely uncontaminated and I am sure you will agree that it will do no harm to the health of juveniles."

"Juveniles indeed! It's not their health I'm

talking about, it's their trespassing on my uncle's land. Who is in charge of this camp?"

"As a matter of fact I am. My name is Sylvanus Specter. I happen to be the owner of Blackbrae and of the land around it, being the heir to my grandfather, the previous owner."

"What absolute nonsense! My uncle bought this place two years ago. It belongs to him."

"And have you the title-deeds, or does your uncle hold them?"

"Of course he has them . . ." Robin was none too sure what was meant by title-deeds, but he gathered some sort of legal document to prove ownership was called for.

"Blackbrae is of very little account to me," said Sylvanus Specter, smiling a wintry smile. "It is a poor cottage. I would willingly give it up entirely to your uncle if he would give up to me my rights as the heir to a far greater estate, the lands in Northumberland, the property of my late grandmother, Mrs. Kezieh Specter, who died in this house seven years ago."

"He's crackers!" whispered Howard. "Grandfathers and grandmothers and him heir to their property. He's got a bee in his bonnet."

Sylvanus Specter surveyed him without resentment.

"I mean no harm to you two boys," he said

gently. "Only you must keep out of my way." He pushed them aside and proceeded to fill his bucket at the spring.

"You may have that pailful," said Robin, seething with inward fury, but trying to remain calm outwardly, "but I am not going to allow your campers to trespass in my uncle's garden, or in his house. So that's final."

"We shall do exactly as we like," said Sylvanus Specter. He walked coolly back to the camp, not spilling a drop though the pail was filled to the brim.

Mrs. MacTaggart came steaming up the hill just then, with wee Jeannie clutching her mother's hand and staring in alarm at the campful of boys. The poor kid must have thought she was seeing an army of ghosts!

"I came along to see if you were all right," said the mother. "My husband has come back early from his work at the farm. Someone telephoned him there to say his old mother is ill, very bad indeed. She wants us all to go to Dumfries at once, so I shall not be here to see to you in the morning. It is a mercy that this camp has arrived today, for you will not be lonesome now. The camp leader came to see us a few minutes ago and he promised to keep an eye on you. A very pleasant-spoken man he is too."

She had thoughtfully brought along a bannock and some oat-cakes and a dozen eggs, and she pointed out the way to the farm, for they would have to fetch their own milk until the Mac-Taggarts returned. Then off she hastened, her whole mind busy with the transporting of her family to Dumfries. A few minutes later the MacTaggart car chugged up the lane and passed out of sight, mother, father and children all waving goodbye.

"Fishy!" said Howard, "very fishy!"

Robin said nothing. His heart descended into his boots, at least that was how he felt. The cheery MacTaggart mum and dad had been like a safe harbour for a ship at sea. Wee Jeannie might fear her ghosties and the old woman by the phone box might utter dark hints, but there was no nonsense about Mr. and Mrs. MacTaggart. Now the two MacTaggarts had gone and there had been no time to ask questions about the family who had once lived at Blackbrae and whose descendant, Sylvanus Specter, claimed to be its lawful owner.

"We are on our own now," he said.

Howard pointed to the camp. "No, we are not. That must be the camp leader she spoke of and he's coming here. We can tell him about that cheeky Specter fellow . . . Spectre . . . So that is why they kept ragging about ghosts!"

The man's face was vaguely familiar to Robin, he could not think why, for he did not remember ever having seen the camp leader before. He had rather piercing eyes, but otherwise looked pleasant enough.

"You are Mr. Chesney's nephew Robin, are you not? And who is this chap? Hunt, ah yes. I am in charge of this camp. Call me George, they all do . . . I know your uncle very well, Robin. Have known him since I was your age. We went to the same school in fact. He put me on to this site for the camp. Told me about you and asked me to let you join in our sports. D'you play football? We are getting up a team. Where do you play?"

"I don't like football, except watching it," said Howard. Robin did like football, very much, but he did not say so. His eyes were watchful.

"We shall be having a sing-song tonight round the camp fire. You will join us, I hope. Pop music of course. Bring along your guitar, or just come and sing. Supper will be cooked over the fire and I can tell you it will be tasty. Tomorrow we go sailing from Berwick. I can take anyone brave enough to risk sea-sickness, and you two look likely lads to me. I hope you will take part in everything, both of you. Come with me and meet the boys."

"Thanks a lot," replied Robin. "Your camp sounds very—well, very jolly, but Hunt and I have work to do. We have come here on purpose to help my uncle. We shall be very busy whitewashing the scullery tonight."

"Hunt does not look the type for house decorating. Not too strong, is he? Open-air life is what he needs. Do him good."

Howard's hackles rose. He hated to be considered delicate. The idea of whitewashing the scullery was as new to him as to Robin, and it was exceedingly distasteful, but he was not going to sing pop songs in the open air in the damp evening for the improvement of his health.

"I'm not musical," he growled. "And I'm a bad sailor. Besides, I don't like that fellow Specter. He's a cheek, claiming this house and tramping all over the garden. Some of your campers went charging all over the cabbage patch we dug up this morning. They're trespassing."

"Well, as a matter of fact young Sylvanus has right on his side. This little place ought to be his, but I cannot discuss that with you. We can have it out with your uncle when he comes back. Meanwhile, let us all be good friends and that includes the Ghost as we call him. He won't bite. Let him browse among your books and he will be mild as a lamb."

George departed after a farewell speech in which he repeated his invitation to partake of all the entertainments provided for his boys. Robin hastened into the kitchen and began rummaging in the drawer under the table. From there he produced a large padlock and key.

"I shall lock the garden gate," he announced. "That fellow is a crook. Uncle Joseph did not tell him about me or ask him to let me join in the sports, because he did not know whether it was Dad or I who was coming, and he had mixed me up with my brother who died four years before I was born. That George is a wrong 'un. His camp's phoney. He wants to get you and me mucking in with those boys and singing round the camp fire or being sick in their boats, while he and Specter ransack this house."

"Is there anything worth stealing?" asked Howard doubtfully.

"Not that I know of. There must be some reason why Sylvanus Specter has been prowling round and making people talk about ghosts and annoying Uncle Joseph."

"I suppose your uncle is all right, is he? I mean that day when we met in Norwich, you did happen to mention that he wangled your grand-father's money. I don't mean to be insulting, but you did say. . . ."

"That was quite different. He had a right to that money because it came from his mother. Dad's Mum, my grandma, was the second wife. Naturally the first one left her money to her own son. My grandma gets a bit niggly about it, but Dad says the will was perfectly just and fair."

"Then there must be something valuable hidden in this house that Specter knows about but can't find. Either your uncle has carried it off with him, or it is still here. Let's look for it."

"More hidden treasure! No thanks."

What else but look for treasure was there to do? Outside the sun still shone and the campers were playing football. Indoors all was gloomy and dark with closed shutters and dim candle-light, oil being such a nuisance in lamps, blackening the glass chimneys and sending sooty fumes everywhere.

Howard discovered an aged copy of *The Boy's Own Book of Indoor Recreations*. Its cover was broken and slit as with a penknife, but inside there were many suggestions for passing the time: ventriloquism, juggling, tricks and puzzles, conjuring and model-making.

Ventriloquism went fairly well until some lout listening by the back door took up the idea and began to mock the ventriloquisors. Juggling ended disastrously in a wholesale smash-up of

Uncle Joseph's tumblers. Most of the tricks and puzzles were fairly obvious and old chestnuts. The conjuring and model-making both required apparatus not to be found in Blackbrae.

In the farthest recesses of the long cupboard beneath the stairs Robin found a violin. It was so old that Howard declared it to be a Stradivarius, an instrument of such value that George and Sylvanus might consider the expense of organizing a camp worthwhile in order to get hold of the thing. Neither of the boys had any knowledge of violin playing and no other musical instrument is so disagreeable to hear as a fiddle attacked for the first time by a learner. Even a Stradivarius could hardly be expected to produce beautiful sounds in the hands of an unmusical boy, and the Blackbrae violin was no Strad. Before long the campers were banging on doors and windows, asking who was torturing the cat, or were they killing a pig? The violin was a dismal failure.

With reluctance the would-be musicians gave up the attempt and settled down to a session on Magic Figures and Numerical Triangles.

They were engaged on this form of mathematical entertainment when a loud determined knock sounded on the front door.

Chapter 8

STATE OF SIEGE

THE knocking continued at intervals for several minutes. Somebody called, "Hi, Rob! Robin Chesney, are you there?" but the voice was muffled by being shouted through the letter-box, and Robin and Howard had taken themselves and their mathematical problems upstairs at the first knock.

"Let him shout and knock all night. I'm not opening the door."

Supper-time and its pangs of hunger brought the boys down at last when the knocking had ceased. Passing through the hall, Robin took a squint through the letter-box to see if his enemies were still lying in wait.

An eye on the other side of the door met his through the slit.

"I say, Chesney old man, can we have a parley? It's important."

"Good night, George!" replied Robin not too politely.

"Listen. Have you heard the weather forecast tonight? There's going to be a bad storm, thunder

6

and lightning and gales force twelve. I've got fifty boys out here and some of them are only kids, under ten, two under eight. I'm not asking you to house the whole crowd of us. We can make do in the stable and barn. If you would let those youngsters in, you'd be doing a good turn. They will sleep on the floor. They all have sleeping-bags. Be a sport, old chap. Half a dozen small boys can't do any harm. You need not be afraid of them."

The last sentence was rather tactless and spoilt the effect of the appeal. However, Robin was not altogether heartless. He had seen a lowering yellow look in the sky when peeping from the bedroom window. He had also seen a couple of kids who did not look a day over six years old crying and rubbing their hands as if they were cold. He would be a selfish beast if he left those two out in the storm.

"The horse!" whispered Howard, clutching his arm.

"Horse? What horse?"

"The Wooden Horse. The Greeks besieged Troy and they could not get inside the walls so they made a wooden horse . . . you know the tale. The Trojans pulled the horse into the city and there were Greeks inside and they captured Troy."

A history lesson delivered when the enemy is negotiating through the letter-box is hardly appropriate. Robin did not see the point.

"The gate," urged Howard. "The Trojans had to take down the gate of the city to get the horse in. . . ."

Gate! That rang a bell in Robin's mind. He had so carefully padlocked the garden gate, yet all evening boys had been prowling round the house, shouting insults, knocking at the door, banging on the windows. Even the leader of the camp, George himself, was on the threshold at this moment. That gate must have been broken open, taken right off its hinges, because the top of the wall was studded with chipped glass stuck in cement. Uncle Joseph or the late owners of Blackbrae had also wished to keep out intruders.

Those small kids were rather overdoing the blubbering. Showing off maybe, and perfectly aware that someone was watching from behind the bedroom curtains. Once get little smarties like that into the house and they'd be like the Greeks inside the horse. . . . Thanks a lot, Howard!

"Hey George! You've got a good van. Why don't you take your babies down to Haddington and park them in a hotel or a nursery school. We don't want hijackers here. You can't kid us.

Didn't you see the padlock on the gate? That was a hint. Keep out!"

"Oh ho! So it's a declaration of war?"

Robin snapped down the flap of the letter-box.

From the window of the small bedroom Howard watched the campers streaming into the stables and lighting a fire in the barn. From the front room, Robin was inspecting the damage done to the gate.

"While they are all round at the back, I could slip out at the front and nip down to the telephone by the old woman's cottage. I ought to ring the police. Housebreaking is a criminal offence and sleeping in somebody's barn is just as bad."

Howard objected strongly to this plan.

"We don't want the police here. My folk will be hopping mad if I get mixed up with police business. Besides, think of your uncle."

"That's exactly what I am thinking of. He told me to keep all boys out of his property."

"You let me in. Suppose Blackbrae does not belong to him. He may have done a fiddle over the money when he bought the place. Your grandma may be right about him being a sharper. You don't want to send your uncle to prison for robbing Sylvanus Specter, do you?"

"O.K. Forget it. I only hope this gang will clear off without doing any damage. They may burn the barn and the stables and themselves too, but Blackbrae is quite strong. These stone walls are about four feet thick."

The knocking at the front door began again, but Robin and Howard ignored it and proceeded to cook their supper. Mrs. MacTaggart's egg and bacon pie was good, but had not quite such a delicious aroma as that of the supper being prepared in the barn. Howard declared that the campers were feasting on roast goose and apple sauce.

By the time supper was finished, the opportunity for escaping to the telephone was past too. The campers, waiting while their goose was cooking (or possibly hare), had congregated in the front garden and someone appeared to be telling them a story, and a funny one too, for there were frequent outbursts of raucous laughter. The distant roll of thunder and occasional spattering of rain did not interrupt them. The boys in the kitchen felt horribly frustrated at not knowing what was going on.

"They're all at the front now," suggested Robin. "I'll slip round from the back and find out what they are up to. You keep the door and let me in as soon as I bang three times on it."

The cooks in the barn were busy with their preparations and did not notice Robin glide silently past. All was still in the yard, though the ladder had been taken from the stable and propped up against the back of the house. Someone had climbed up on the roof. Robin had to find out why, so he went up too.

For a moment the clouds raced by, leaving the clear moonlight. By it, he saw a great white sheet, tied at its four corners to the two chimney-pots, making a sail which billowed in the wind. Some words were painted on the sheet but he could not read them from the back in this uncertain light. He had to go down the ladder again and creep round to the side, then hide behind the shrubby bushes where he could both see and hear.

Sylvanus Specter was standing on the roof relating the end of a story, the story of two unfortunate stowaways. . . . Robin did not need to see what was written on the sheet though the huge letters were daubed in scarlet paint:

PATAGONIA VIA RUSSIA

So Sylvanus Specter knew; George, that oily camp leader knew; all the campers who had laughed and jeered knew. If that sheet remained on the roof in the morning, the postman would know, and anybody else who happened to pass that way. Rob would be in the papers again and on the telly and all Norwich would find out. To be made a figure of fun is the worst kind of suffering. Ridicule is harder to bear with fortitude than pain.

He sneaked humbly round to the back door and knocked three times. Howard let him in very fast indeed, slamming the door behind him and bolting it tightly.

"Someone came while you were away. He only knocked once but I thought it was you so I began to open up. Then he said in a sort of hoarse whisper, 'Let me in. I'm on your side,' so I pushed him out and locked up again. I remembered another thing about those Greeks. It's a sort of proverb. Beware of the Greeks when they bring gifts. It means they pretend to be your friend and then let you down."

"They know about us going to Russia. That Specter has got the whole camp jeering like mad and he's put up a whacking great poster on the roof for everyone to see, a huge sheet painted in red, Patagonia via Russia. We shall never live that down, never."

The insistent knocking on the door changed to a thunderous clamour. Someone was trying to force his way in and between the blows came angry shouting and threats.

"Open this door at once or it will be the worse for you," was the mildest of the menaces. Abuse, swearing and sneers shouted through the letter-box were accompanied by handfuls of pebbles and bits of lighted paper which the boys could not ignore.

As suddenly as it had begun, the noise ceased and the voice of George could be heard, loud, but decisive, ordering the campers to go round to the big barn where supper was ready.

"No more racket here, boys. I will deal with the fellows in the house."

The silence that followed was even more unnerving than the uproar.

"D'you think they mean to murder us?" asked Howard, a quaver in his voice. "I don't want to die."

"Murder? Of course not. Murderers don't bring along fifty boys as witnesses. No, they want to steal something belonging to my uncle, but I don't know what it is. First they tried to get us out of the way while they searched for it and now they are trying to frighten us, so that we shall try to escape by the front door while the campers are at supper. But we won't go. They can't break down that heavy oak door. The walls are too thick to burn down. If they have explosives they may try to blow us up, but then they'd lose whatever they are trying to find. So there's nothing to worry about. They'll be singing pop-songs soon round the camp fire in the barn, and smoking too I expect. He may keep that lot quiet with drugs, I shouldn't wonder."

Howard shivered. Robin's well-meant advice did not have the intended result. He could picture George and Sylvanus creeping round in the dark with sticks of gelignite and fuses while their two innocent victims were asleep. Those rowdy, impudent campers were detestable, but at least they were alive. Infinitely worse would be a barnful of drugged imbeciles, dreaming and helpless in the disused farm buildings unaware of anything but their own hallucinations. He and Robin might scream for help, but nobody would stir. Then when morning came George and Sylvanus would have disappeared with their treasure and the pathetic murder of the two inmates of Blackbrae would be accounted for as the result of drug-taking.

To go to bed was unthinkable. They stirred up the fire and made some more cocoa, hot and sweet.

"They may kill us if they get in," said Howard. "I don't know anything about dying, Rob. It's funny but my folks won't talk about dying. They say it is morbid to even think about it. But we have all got to die, so we ought to know what happens and how to be ready for death. My mum and dad were not allowed to talk about sex when they were kids, so they told me about that years ago, but not about death. I know that our bodies decay so they have to be burnt or buried. They are no more important dead than teeth which come out and are thrown away, or arms and legs which have to be amputated. But the rest of us, the real person, where does it go? I read a verse once written by Hadrian, the Roman chap who built the wall between England and Scotland. He wrote it on his death-bed:

> 'Fickle, roving, charming sprite,
> The body's guest and comrade bright,
> Whither goest thou, to what shore?
> Naked, chilly, deathly white. . . .
> All thy youthful jests are o'er.' "

Robin stared in amazement.

"What a queer stick you are, How! Fancy you thinking up all that about dying. I don't expect to die till I'm about ninety. My mum says you go to Heaven if you are good and Dad says the other place if you are bad, and 'Take care not to have an accident, son.' Grandma says, 'Wait and see.' "

"I hoped you could help me. But you are just the same as everyone else. They all try to jolly me along into believing it won't happen, like the ostrich burying its head in the sand. But dying does happen, and I want to know how to live that I shall be ready to die."

Robin felt hot round the collar and a bit creepy. He much preferred the ostrich way of facing death.

"I suppose we ought to say some prayers, only I don't know any. I'm not up in that sort of thing."

Somewhere in the upper part of the house something heavy fell with a clatter. Robin thought perhaps Sylvanus was taking down his poster on the roof.

"I don't know how to pray either," said Howard. "We don't go to church in our family. But I will do my best and perhaps God will understand." He closed his eyes and said earnestly;

"Please God, we've been following a wrong map again and we are in a jam. We don't know what to do. Will you help us."

Robin said "Amen", which he knew was a good ending for a prayer. He was not sure what it meant, but "That's for me too" was in his mind.

More strange sounds came from above, a banging, a crash of falling plaster.

"It's coming down from the roof. . . . They've made a hole and they are getting through."

"It's like the Siege of Quebec," muttered Howard. "When Wolfe couldn't conquer the city any other way, he climbed up the Heights of Abraham and came down from above."

"You and your history lessons!" shouted Robin. "Come on. We must drive them back."

Chapter 9

INVASION

UNDER the roof lay a long narrow garret, stretching from one end of the house to the other. Robin had explored it on his first day at Blackbrae and had considered it to be without interest. The garret was reached from the passage outside the bedrooms by a ladder going up to a trap-door, rather heavy and awkward to open from below. There was nothing in the garret but a couple of empty suitcases and a disused cistern. As a room, the place was useless, because the floor consisted of rafters set quite far apart with plaster in between. The slope of the roof formed its walls and there was no skylight to dispel the darkness.

The trap-door had been the only means of entry until Sylvanus Specter, fixing his impudent poster between the chimneys had thought of the idea of removing some of the slates and making a hole in the roof.

Robin and Howard made a desperate attempt to drag the ladder off its hooks, to prevent the invaders getting any farther than the garret, but the ladder was firmly fixed in place and would not budge. Showers of rubble clattered down, cracking the plaster of the landing ceiling, and two thuds above warned them that entry had already been made into the garret. Then someone drew up the hatch, and Sylvanus dropped easily down ignoring the ladder completely. George followed more cautiously but too quickly to allow time for the defenders to put up a fight. He rubbed the dust off his clothes and smiled.

"Don't be alarmed, boys. We mean no harm whatever to either of you. All we want is to search this house and to find something which is of value to my young cousin Sylvanus, and of no value at all to your uncle or to anyone else. It is unfortunate that you turned up this weekend when the house should have been empty and we could have made our investigations in peace. Finding that you were to be here, we took the trouble of bringing along a campful of other boys to entertain you, but you two have proved un-cooperative and have obstinately refused to join in with their activities. Time is getting short now and we can play around no longer. We are going to put you out of our way in the front bedroom which Sylvanus has already searched thoroughly. If you make a noise, no one will hear. The campers are all at the back of the house and are already making enough din to drown your shouts. Now hustle. Into the bedroom with you."

They fought hard, kicking, and biting when the enemy pinioned their arms, but Sylvanus was big and strong, and his cousin was amazingly tough. Howard's glasses were knocked off and trampled on in the struggle. He could not see much without them, so that put him out of action. George tied him to a chair and gagged him while Robin struggled on with Sylvanus until he in turn was overcome.

Uncommonly foolish they felt as they sat with their hands tied behind them and their legs bound at the ankles, gags in their mouths and both of them aching and bruised. George hurried off to begin his search but Sylvanus sat down on the end of the bed and surveyed his captives.

"You are a couple of cranks," he said. "Can't you see that you've not a hope of winning? I told you before that this house is mine by right, but I am after bigger game than Blackbrae.

"My grandmother was heiress to a vast property in the north of England. She held the title-deeds, but she was a poor simple body and dared not claim her rights. Her husband, my grandfather, would not believe that she could ever inherit the lands of her ancestors. She was afraid of her husband and she hid the title-deeds here in this house, meaning to keep them for her son, my father. My dad died without ever finding those deeds and I am his heir. When the old lady died, her cruel husband turned my father out of the house and he left it to a distant relation who sold it to your uncle. But he did not destroy those title-deeds. He hid them. A legal document of that kind is no use to you or to your uncle, only to me. I want to be rich and powerful. I want to own wealth and lands. I want money. And I am going to get it."

He stood up, scowling and kicking angrily at the bedpost. "If my grandfather had left this house to me, as he ought, then I should have had plenty of opportunity of finding that legal document. Mr. Chesney was quite decent at first and he listened when I explained about the title-deeds, but he turned nasty and said he would not have me poking about his house.

"What's he got to hide, if it isn't my title-deeds? Why does he fill the place with books, not the kind of historical books he reads, medieval law and such, but any old tripe, novels and kids' stories and travel and bound volumes of magazines fifty years out of date? He wants to hide something. He wants me to spend hours taking off the covers to see if my deeds are hidden inside and draw me away from the real hiding-place.

"My grandfather never destroyed the document. He said on his deathbed, 'I have not destroyed my wife's precious treasure. I hadn't the heart to burn it, when the poor old soul put such store by it.' The nurse in the hospital wrote those words down for me, so I know. The treasure is here in Blackbrae. My father came back night after night to get it, and since he died, I have come too. And I intend to find it tonight, whatever happens."

The ghost-boy glared at his two captives and departed, slamming the door behind him.

Robin and Howard winked at one another which was all they could do, imprisoned as they were. To talk was impossible, and all their efforts were centred on wriggling out of their bonds. In a television play, a broken bottle would have turned up conveniently with which to cut the cords, but the big bedroom held no broken bottles and neither boy could reach his pen-knife. Robin tried to move his chair nearer to the candle, hoping to be able to burn the cord at his wrists. He only succeeded in knocking the candle over, plunging them both in darkness which was all the more depressing because the lightning flashed from time to time. The growling thunder and pouring rain combined to add to their misery.

7

Robin thought dismally of Howard's prayer. Did God hear prayers, he wondered. Perhaps they had not prayed the right way. People who were religious and who went to church would have known how to speak to God. Well, he and Howard were in a jam once more. Sylvanus had a chip on his shoulder about not being rich, envious of more fortunate folk. Perhaps that made him a bit crazy, for he was not such a bad fellow otherwise. That George now, he had been far more brutal, smashing poor old Howard's glasses on purpose. What had he to get out of this business of Sylvanus and his lost inheritance? He would not back up the ghost unless he had something to gain. That fellow would expect to make a handsome profit out of anything he undertook. He must know that great estates are not inherited without a lot of fuss with lawyers and the peculiar language they use, probate and all that, legal forms, signed and sealed and witnessed, parchment generally, very heavy and important.

He wriggled his jaws, trying to bite through the piece of sheet torn up to make gags. Uncle Joseph's sheets seemed made of extremely tough material . . . might even be parchment. Parchment . . . Tom Hopkins' map.

It was not a map he and Howard needed now.

It was a person, someone to come and set them free.

On the opposite side of the room, Howard sat in the darkness, anxiously trying to work his hands free, but only succeeding in cutting his wrists with the hard cord that bound them. He felt hopeless, despairing, convinced that his last hour had come.

In the roof hole the torrential rain brought down another heap of rubble, which clattered on the bedroom ceiling. The scrabbling which followed made Howard think of rats, adding to his terror. Were they to be eaten alive, helpless and alone in the dark? He could not pray aloud now, but pray he did, most earnestly.

A thud up above and then soft movements. With a gentle squeak the key turned in the lock. Cautiously somebody opened the door and flashed the light of a torch over the two unhappy prisoners. A voice spoke, quietly but cheerfully:

"Hi, chums! Here's Tom Hopkins. This time I've come to get you OUT OF A MESS, not into one!"

He lit the candle, untied the gags and freed first hands and then feet.

"So now we've got to escape. We can do the talking later. We must not make a sound."

He took off his shoes, tied them together by the laces and slung them round his neck.

Robin made for the window, but Tom held him back.

"We can't climb down that tree. Too tricky in the dark. The roof's no use. It's wet and slippery. We must go out by the front door. Follow me."

Chapter 10

ESCAPE

FRIEND or foe? Robin crept downstairs uncertain how to take this sudden appearance of Thomas Hopkins. Was he one of the boys in the camp? Had he told the tale of his wretched treasure-map to Sylvanus Specter? He knew where to find the prisoners, so he must be on the side of the enemy. Yet if he was working for George and Sylvanus, why release their captives?

Not for a moment did Robin consider disobeying Tom's orders, though. Tom had set them free. Tom knew what he was about.

The kitchen door was shut but ominous sounds came from within, as if George and Sylvanus were engaged on breaking up the happy home. From the hammering and crashing that was going on, it seemed that the two were prising the shelves from the walls, scattering cups and plates, jugs and saucers to the ground in frantic haste.

The three boys reached the front door in safety and Robin carefully drew back the bolts top and bottom. Then he gasped in horror. The door was locked as well and the key had been removed.

"In here!" Robin opened the parlour door. If they could take down the shutters without making too much noise, they could escape through the window. The piano, drawn sideways across a corner, offered a temporary hiding-place if they made too much row and disturbed the searchers. The shutters proved awkward and the boys were still fumbling with the heavy bar when the door of the kitchen opened.

By the light of the oil lamp on the kitchen table, they could see George on his knees before a cupboard which he was ransacking, heaving out the contents, old saucepan lids, washing powder, tea-towels, cutlery, cake-tins and patty-pans. Sylvanus, wielding a broom, swept the lot into the hall and returned to his own job, that of hacking with a pickaxe at the wall beside the range. The shower of loose bricks he brought down deadened the sound of three boys scrambling in great haste behind one upright piano.

"The kitchen is a complete wash-out!" declared Sylvanus, inspecting the damage he had done. "The old man must have hidden it in the parlour after all. I've looked there. It is not in the piano or the bookcase or in the china-cupboard. We must rip up that old horse-hair sofa and the two armchairs. But that's too obvious. I'm convinced that there's a secret hiding-place in the walls, covered with paper to hide it, those hideous faded roses, just what she would have used."

They carried in the lamp and proceeded to slit open the upholstery of the chairs and sofa, but in vain. Peeling off layer after layer of aged wallpaper revealed no secret cupboard. "It's in the bedrooms," said George. "I told you so all along. An old dame wishing to hide something always hides it in her bedroom. I've had enough experience to know that."

"I've been through all the cupboards and wardrobes and chests of drawers. Old Chesney put in new bedding, mattresses and all, the only thing he did buy for Blackbrae. Still we could try the walls. What about those two kids?"

Robin held his breath. If George and Sylvanus would only go upstairs without any more talk, they would leave the way free for a dash to the back door. The rubbish piled on the floor would be a nuisance, but . . .

At that most inconvenient moment, Howard sneezed. He had been holding back that sneeze for some moments, and when it came it came in triplicate, loud and long.

Sylvanus, who had just reached the first step of the stairs, came racing back into the parlour and made straight for the piano, the only article of furniture which could offer any concealment. The first person he hauled out was Tom.

"He's a spy!" he shouted. "He's one of the Youth Club. I saw him with the campers by the gate."

"Not at all," said Tom with a laugh, brushing a spider off his coat. "Far from being a spy, I happen to be an old schoolmate of these two chaps and I was just about to call on Rob Chesney when I saw you hoisting a sheet on the roof. Naturally I paused to watch such an unusual proceeding. Afterwards I knocked at the front door and at the back door, but could get no reply. Then I went down to Innernuik telephone kiosk and rang up my father to tell him that I was intending to spend the night here. He has business in Edinburgh and will be along tomorrow to pick me up."

"We don't want your life-history," growled Sylvanus. "How did you get in here?"

"Same as you, through the roof. I saw a ladder and went up."

Thomas Hopkins was not short and stocky like Robin, nor pale and overgrown like Howard. He was now as tall as Sylvanus and as powerfully built. He did not quail before the wrathful George but faced him calmly.

"Hadn't you better clear off, you two?" he

said. "My father may come tonight and this house is in rather a mess."

George changed his tactics. He was once again the pleasant-spoken camp leader who had impressed Mrs. MacTaggart with his care for the boys in his charge.

"My dear boy, you are mistaken. We have full permission from Mr. Chesney to carry on these investigations. Your young pals have really no right to be in this house at all. If you found them tied up, it was merely to keep them out of the way of falling bricks. Now I will make a perfectly fair offer. If these boys will show me what they have found and I know that they have found something or they would not have barricaded the house in this way, I say if they will give in and show us their discovery, we shall set them free and you too, my dear boy."

"I am not your dear boy and I very much doubt if these two chaps have made any discovery at all. They look completely bewildered."

"We have not found anything," declared Robin. "I have never seen anything in this house that I would give fivepence for in a jumble sale."

"There's a silver candlestick in the bedroom," suggested Howard hopefully.

Sylvanus scowled. "Not that sort of thing. I

told you what I am looking for. It is a document, the title-deeds of my estate."

"In a box," added George. "Old Specter said it was in a box."

Howard's short-sighted eyes gleamed. "We did find a box in the garden—buried it was. Rather like a small coffin."

"But it—" Robin's exclamation broke off short. If they could only reach freedom in the open air! Once those fellows got digging up that stick in a box, there'd be a chance of escape. Nobody can dig for buried treasure and guard prisoners at the same time.

"I didn't like the idea of opening it," said Robin. "We thought there might be a skeleton inside. It was buried deep but we were giving the cabbage-bed a real double-digging, not just scratching on the top as my uncle did when he planted the cabbages. We will show you the place and you can dig up the box."

"One of you only. This one." George selected Howard and pushed him towards the kitchen.

"You smashed his glasses. He can't see! I'm coming too."

"You will all three come and you will do the digging," said George. Digging a wet and muddy cabbage-bed in the dark is unpleasant work, suitable for captives, not for their captors.

The storm had passed by the time the second exhumation of the box began, but the earth was soggy with the rain though the feet of many campers had trampled it in the past few hours. The boys in the stables had gone to bed and they had pitched their fire-pan out on the grass where the last remains fizzled and smouldered. This second digging was much harder than the first, but at last the old box came into sight.

Robin leaped out of the hole and Tom heaved Howard after him.

"It's wet and mouldy and there may be a corpse in it," objected Tom, who was still rather bewildered by the curious goings-on at Black-brae, though he had got the message all right about the escape. "It may be a corpse or a skeleton, but on the other hand it might be a treasure. If it is a treasure, the owner should be the one to open the box, and make the first inspection."

"Get out of my way!" Sylvanus pushed every-one aside and jumped into the hole, followed very smartly by George, and together they began to heave up the box. Their prisoners did not wait for the opening ceremony. They took to their heels and ran.

They were almost at the top of the hill, where the lane turned into a secondary road, when an outburst of violent swearing made them look back. In the faint moonlight they could see Sylvanus Specter brandishing the pole.

"A witch's broomstick and nothing else," he screamed as he broke the pole several times across his knee and tossed it on the smouldering remains of the camp fire. He did not trouble to follow his escaped prisoners, but just stood, utterly disconsolate, staring at the sparks which arose from the broken stick.

Muddy and dishevelled, the three boys struggled up to the turning. The cottages at Innernuik seemed the only refuge, but there was a long way to go. They had not covered much ground before Howard, half-blinded without his glasses, tripped over a clump of grass on the side of the road and fell headlong.

"Go on!" he pleaded. "Don't wait for me. I can't run. Go and get help."

Chapter 11

LIVERY OF SEISIN

TO desert Howard was quite out of the question. He had a sprained ankle, he would not be able to stagger as far as the telephone, so Rob and Tom heaved him to the side of the road and prepared to do battle.

But the battle appeared to be engaged in the rear. George's voice bellowed away back in the garden, "You young fool! Where's the cash?"

"Cash? There's no cash. Grandfather lived on his pension. He had no money. It's the documents I'm after. I told you."

A burst of swearing showed that George had heard from other sources that the old man was a miser; that Sylvanus was pulling a fast one about ancient documents; the boy was after a hidden hoard. Sounds of a struggle ensued, and a few minutes later the large van which had brought the campers was driven out of the lane by a thunderous-looking George, who did not trouble to glance at his former captives.

"He's lost a pound note, and found fivepence," muttered Robin. "Whatever that crook was searching for it wasn't title-deeds of a lost estate. Hullo! What's that?"

"That" was a distant jarring of brakes and the screech of two cars, followed by voices raised in anger.

"George has bashed into somebody. Hope it isn't your dad."

"My dad would not be swearing like that! Well, they can't be much hurt as they are kicking up such a row!"

"I believe," said Robin, "I am not sure, but I think that the man George has crashed into is my Uncle Joseph."

"Well I hope your Uncle Joseph hasn't got a weak heart. If he has, he will have a coronary thrombosis or something when he sees his home. Two shocks in one night might finish him."

Robin sighed. "He will finish me, more likely. He left me his house to look after, and I tried my best but that wasn't enough. He warned me not to let boys in, and I could not keep them out."

"Sylvanus Specter the Ghost is probably still there, knocking holes in the walls," said Howard. "I think his precious document must have been thrown on the fire ages ago."

Joseph Chesney's car chugged up the hill, its bumpers buckled and scratched. The occupant, though naturally vexed, was not injured except in his feelings. He drew up at the sight of the three boys, very angry indeed.

"What does this mean, you lads knocking around here in the middle of the night? Be off with you! Hey, you there, are you my nephew Stephen? No! Robin? You ought to be in your bed."

"Burglars, Uncle Joseph. They broke in through the roof. These two chaps are friends of mine. There's been a whole campful of boys all for Specter."

"Specter is it? Ha! I know Sylvanus. If you had arrived on time, nephew, as you should have done, I could have made a better arrangement. Your train got in soon after four a.m. Yet you did not come until after four p.m. You will have to explain that delay, but not now. Hop in, all of you."

On the whole, Uncle Joseph's cardiac condition must have been fairly sound. He surveyed the deserted tents, flapping in the wind, the shuttered house with its adornment on the roof, the gate lying flat on the grass and the camp fire, now beginning to blaze merrily, in the garden. And he did not say a word.

He produced his own key for the front door and entered his week-end cottage to see the hall littered with broken china, kitchen utensils, coverless books, strips of wallpaper and broken bricks. His small sitting-room was a shambles; the kitchen a nightmare. On the bottom step of the stairs sat Sylvanus Specter, his head in his hands, a picture of misery. Above on the landing a crowd of inquisitive boys peered down.

"What's goin' on?" inquired one lad. "Mr. George, he's took off the van and done a bunk. So that woke us up and we couldn't make anyone hear in the house, so we climbed up the ladder and came through the roof. What's up? Have someone been murdered or what? We heard some shoutin'."

Uncle Joseph uttered a small groan. He disliked boys, finding them noisy, impudent, inquisitive and self-opinionated. Never in his wildest dreams had he imagined such a horror as a houseful of the creatures! But, as his half-brother had observed, he was not completely hard-hearted, and the sight of the cheeky, insolent Sylvanus heart-broken with disappointment stirred within him some vague pity. For the other boys, whoever they might be, he had only one word to say. He opened the front door again and said it:

"OUT!"

The campers, carefully avoiding the disconsolate Specter, trooped down the stairs and
returned to their sleeping-bags, awed and puzzled.
When they had all gone, Mr. Chesney turned to
Sylvanus and tapped him on the shoulder.

"Now what have you been up to?"

The boy raised his eyes, half defiant, half
ashamed.

"I've done what I told you I would. I have
smashed up the whole place and I have searched
everywhere."

"And you found nothing?"

"Nothing. Now then, say it. Tell me again that
you said all along there was nothing to find."

Mr. Chesney shrugged his shoulders. "Robin,
my lad, just look in the kitchen and find out if
there are any cups left. I think a pot of tea might
be acceptable, even though the hour is past midnight. And if you can rustle up anything to eat
so much the better. Take your friends with you
and try to clear a space and prepare a meal.
Sylvanus Specter and I have matters to discuss."

While the discussion went on in the hall, Tom
practised First Aid on Howard's ankle, and Robin
boiled a kettle and cut thick slices of bread and
butter. He had often noticed such ordinary fare
tasted infinitely more exotic when consumed in

8

the middle of the night. (His mother was afraid of thunderstorms, so his dad frequently produced tea and bread and butter in the night.) Howard was not addicted to midnight feasts which were not allowed in his home. Also he disliked tea and bread and butter because they reminded him of his one and only visit to Russia, and the unpleasantness it had caused. Sylvanus drank a cup of tea, and when his talk was ended he went back to the barn to join the other campers there and Uncle Joseph came into the kitchen.

"Well, I deserved this," he said, surveying the mess. "I was on to a good thing, you see. I bought up a second-hand bookshop. The owner knew nothing of books and he had some very fine first editions and a tremendous amount of rubbish. I bought the lot, dirt cheap, scattered the books round the house to give young Specter something to hold up his operations. . . . He has been nagging round seeking his lost title-deeds ever since his father died. Then I got this telegram calling me to Ireland, and I knew I could meet someone there who would give me a good price, but I was fairly sure that the telegram was some of young Specter's doing, or of the man who has organized tonight's business here. I had gathered Sylvanus had chummed up with a criminal type. Young fool, Sylvanus! He's mad about money, but if he does not take care he will be spending his life in the nick instead of in his vast estates.

"Of course there is no legal document, no ancient will, no title-deeds of any sort hidden in this house. I have known the Specter family for years. The old grandmother was a weak shiftless body, the last of an ancient family who had lived in the Border Country for centuries. Maybe they once owned a great domain; the memory of it has survived as a sort of legend. But they must have lost their possessions about the time of the Wars of the Roses, and they will never get them back."

Uncle Joseph yawned and stood up. "There's not much of the night left. We all need a bit of shut-eye. But you see, Robin, why I said I deserved what I have got? When I saw you, I ought to have put off my trip to Ireland, lost my handsome profit, and taken care of the young nephew who had come a long journey in answer to my appeal. Sorry you've had a bad time, lad. A bit of plaster and rubble on the bed does not make much difference to persons too tired to bother with undressing."

Mr. Chesney did not go to bed. He was too busy assessing the damage done and checking his own personal possessions. He was a wealthy man, and had not troubled much about his "little place in the country", because he liked living a simple life from time to time, imagining himself as a man unfettered by the cares and anxieties of the modern technological age. He was also a shrewd business man, determined to get every possible penny from the insurance of Blackbrae, and of his damaged car.

"The only good deed these vandals have done," he announced as he sat watching Tom and Robin prepare the breakfast, "was that they have dug up my cabbage bed. I had been feeling for some time that a garden should make a profit in the way of vegetables. Heavy digging is not my line, however, and gardeners are hard to find nowadays. If you three boys would like to fill in the hole the vandals made, we could have a good crop of spring cabbages in that patch."

"We dug it up twice yesterday," objected Howard. "It's tough work digging and we only found an old box. Wasn't it a giggle when old George and Sylvanus opened the box all frantic with excitement, and found only an old stick. . . ."

"A stick? What kind of a stick?" roared Uncle Joseph.

"It was in a long, narrow box, like a thin coffin," explained Robin. "The box was lined with lead or zinc or something and the stick must have been put there for a joke. It had been buried quite a time."

Uncle Joseph's eyes gleamed. "Out in the garden, boys. Show me this stick at once. Where is it?"

Alas! The stick had smouldered on through the rest of the night, and by morning nothing remained but a heap of ashes. The box was still there, smashed to pieces by a furious hand wielding a spade in wrath.

"The box does not matter. Made no more than a century ago. But the stick! I have no doubt about the stick. Old Specter vowed that his wife had some old family heirloom which gave her the right to a property over the Border. He thought she was daft, and after her death he hid it. That's what everybody thought was a legal document, the famous title-deeds."

"But an old broken stick can't be used for title-deeds. It had no seals on it, no signatures, no witnesses. It was just an old stick. Sylvanus smashed it and tossed the bits on the fire."

"Have you never heard of Livery of Seisin, my boy?" Robin had not. Neither had Howard or Tom or Sylvanus who had slouched out from the barn on hearing voices by the scene of the previous night's disaster.

"You do not know? Bah! No history taught in

schools these days. Seisin is the old legal word for possession. A person who owned property was said to be seized of it. Livery of Seisin meant the handing over of property. In the middle ages, when most people, even among the nobles, could neither read nor write, a business transaction had to be done by tokens. If you gave someone a house, you would hand over a key in token of possession. If you gave him an acre of land, you would first present him with a piece of turf, or a branch of a tree. When a king granted an estate to one of his subjects, he would have a lance broken in two and he would give one half in token of the royal gift. If any dispute as to the ownership of that estate should arise, the true possessor could prove his rights by producing his half lance, which must fit in with the other half in the King's possession. That half lance was what we should call title-deeds today."

Sylvanus Specter stifled a groan.

"That custom became obsolete centuries ago, my boy. The lance would have no value in law today, though intensely interesting from the historical standpoint. It seems incredible that your grandmother's family should have kept it through so many years, but I suppose the significance of the broken lance faded into a legend of lost property, lost position and lost wealth, a dim race memory of a golden age long past. You know the sort of story old people tell, 'Your ancestors fought in the Battle of Agincourt', or 'If you had your rights you'd wear a ducal coronet'. At first, I expect, the lance was guarded as a precious token, but after many hopeless attempts to regain possession of what it stood for, the family probably thought of it as a useless heirloom. But for the fact that old Mrs. Specter's family continued to live in the same remote hamlet, the broken stick would have been tossed on the rubbish heap centuries ago. People move round so much these days.

Some ancestor must have made the lined box to preserve the token, perhaps because he had heard the tale which Mrs. Specter got from her great-grandmother, though the old lady could not recall even the name of the property once owned by the family. Your grandmother, Sylvanus, the last of her tribe, brought the box with her when she married, but her husband thought the story nonsense and refused to allow her to pass on the broken lance to his son. That's my reconstruction of the story."

Mr. Chesney thumped Sylvanus on the shoulder.

"Cheer up, my lad. You are young and strong and you live in a new world. Property is no joke these days. The greater your wealth, the greater your taxation. Forget the past and face up to the future." He added with a twinkle in his shrewd old eyes:

"You'll be glad to know that I do not propose to take any action about what happened here last night. I should have seen through that bogus telegram. I regret letting that scamp of a friend of yours off, but he will doubtless end up in prison without my help. The police are quite capable of rounding him up.

"And as regards those boys out in the camp, I am going to drive over to Haddington and fix up about a coach to transport them all home. Can't have them camping round here with nobody in charge. Where did they come from? Newcastle way? Well, we must get them home safely.

"Now young Tom, what are you looking at me in that kind of way for? Have I said something I should not?"

"No, sir. It's something you have not said. You have explained Sylvanus's story clearly and you have been most generous about him and George and the campers, but what about the man in prison?"

"Eh what? Who? Oh you mean the man whose books I bought? He got a fair price, all I offered."

"But you said you got a big profit on the first editions."

"Business, my boy. Good business."

Tom did not reply. Uncle Joseph went quite red to the ears.

"I suppose I ought to do something about that too," he said ruefully.

Robin began to understand then why his dad always stuck up for Uncle Joseph.

Chapter 12

THE OTHER TREASURE

"WHATEVER has been going on here?" The cheerful face of Mrs. MacTaggart grew pale with horror as she gazed upon the destruction of the kitchen she had tried so hard to keep in good order.

The MacTaggart family had arrived back very early, because they, like Uncle Joseph, had been summoned away on a bogus appeal. Finding her mother-in-law in excellent health, Mrs. Mac-Taggart had demanded who had dared to send for the family to come immediately to the old lady's death-bed? Her husband insisted on staying for one night in his home in Dumfries but they came back early, wondering what mischief was afoot.

"House-breaking," explained Robin with a grin. "I'm afraid the kitchen is not as tidy as it was when I came. Fortunately two of my friends came to my rescue, and one of the burglars turned out to be a friend of my uncle's . . . well, not exactly a friend, but they seem to be good pals now."

Sylvanus looked a bit sheepish. Mrs. Mac-Taggart surveyed him sadly.

"So you've been at your tricks again, laddie. You and your father before you, always seeking what you will never get. But neither the one nor the other of you would have damaged the place on your own. You will have had some bad companions who planned all this. I will be telling my man to take the children home while I try to get the kitchen to rights."

"I'd better take the poster down from the roof," said Sylvanus, mounting the stairs four steps at a time. Naturally the others came too. It is not often that one has the opportunity of scrambling about on a steep slate roof, at least with a perfectly good reason for doing so. The view from the top of Blackbrae was magnificent too, for you could see for miles over the hills to the sea. "Was it true about you two going off to Russia in mistake for Patagonia?" asked Sylvanus, "or did George make up that tale? He said he saw you both on television and he recognized Robin in the train. That's what made him think of suggesting to the Youth Club that they could camp here. It was all done in a hurry, but you see Mr. Chesney did not go away at once, as we expected him to, and George thought he could get rid of Robin easily among a crowd of boys."

He hauled down the offending poster with its insulting reminder of bygone mischief. The fresh white sheet was now a bedraggled, dirty rag, torn by the wind and rain, hideously stained with soot and red paint.

"We could try washing it," suggested Howard. "My mother uses a good detergent in our washing machine."

"The best detergent in the world would not get these stains out or mend the tears," said Sylvanus, rolling the sheet into a ball. "I shall have to buy a new sheet for Mr. Chesney. What a mess I have made! Come on downstairs or one of us will break his neck falling off this steep roof. Howard has already got a bad ankle because of me. I have done enough damage."

They took the sheet down to the garden and made a bonfire for it and for the accumulated rubbish swept up by Mrs. MacTaggart, as well as the books which Uncle Joseph discarded. He was busy sorting through the collection, piling up those which might be worth keeping and tossing the rest out of the window to add to the fire.

"My father will be coming soon to drive me home," said Tom, as he stood watching the blaze, "and what with the siege and the escape and all the events at Blackbrae, I have never said what I came to say."

"You need not bring that up!" said Robin. "We do not ever want to hear about your map again."

Tom heaved an armful of out-of-date glossy magazines on the fire and the flames leaped high.

"It's not digging up the past I came for. It's about the future. There's another treasure for you to find, and this goes for Sylvanus too. I can't give you a map for this journey, but I came to tell you of a Guide who will go with you all the way. After I went to live in Carlisle, Jesus Christ found me and called me to serve Him. He showed me that I was pretty rotten all through. Like that old sheet I was torn and stained. I had never loved God or anybody but myself. I had tricked my best friends and I had made fun of them. And yet in spite of that, God loved me. That began a new life for me. I wanted to tell you the Bible words which have changed my life:

'The Son of God loved me and gave Himself for me.'

"He loved me and He loved you too. He died for me and for you. I just had to tell you, in case you had never thought about it. That's why I chased Rob to Norwich, and when Howard said

Rob did not want to see me, and Howard would not stop to talk, I wangled Rob's address here and got Dad to bring me over when he was going to Edinburgh on business.

"It's tremendously important and I have not much time to explain. But if you read that verse in the second chapter of Galatians, you will see that the new life has to be lived by faith, by believing that Christ died for you. Trusting Him is like . . . well, like claiming an inheritance. His promises are the title-deeds to life eternal. Don't lose the inheritance because you can't be bothered to claim it, like Sylvanus's ancestors."

He broke off because a car was turning down the lane. His father had come to fetch him and he had to say a quick goodbye and hurry away.

Howard watched the car disappear and then he jabbed the bonfire with a stick.

"I want to remember Tom's sermon. He came a long way to preach it, and when he got here we would not let him in. When he did enter he had to fight for us and help us to escape. He only had a few minutes to give us his message. I shall remember it by three Fs. Friend. Fortune. Faith. I like his text, 'The Son of God loved me', because that makes Jesus a Friend, a real Friend who will never get bored with me or give me up, and as He is the Son of God He will be with me when I die and afterwards too."

"I wanted a fortune," said Sylvanus. "I've been wanting it for years. My father wanted it too, but my mother always said that earthly possessions would pass away, and she used to speak of an inheritance which would be eternal. I suppose when Tom began that new life, it was like claiming the eternal inheritance because he believed that text, his title-deeds, 'The Son of God loved me and gave Himself for me.' I wish I could believe that too."

"That's the faith part," said Robin. "Maybe your old ancestors did not believe that the lance really could give them their estates, so they put it away and never brought it to the king, so they never got their inheritance. I hadn't much faith last night, because I was scared stiff, but Howard believed that God would help us, and God did, for He sent Tom to rescue us. I had been so angry with Tom that I wanted never to see him again. He said that God had changed his life and he proved it by coming to help us in the siege and by not being afraid to tell us what God had done for him. I want to have faith enough to believe that the Son of God loved me and gave Himself for me. I want to find Tom's new Treasure."

And then Uncle Joseph put his head out of the window and shouted:

"If you boys have finished burning up the debris, come in and help me to put the house in order."